They Don't Check out

Aaron Thomas Milstead

BLOOD BOUND BOOKS

Copyright © 2015 by Aaron Thomas Milstead

All rights reserved

ISBN 978-1-940250-19-9

Artwork by Andrej Bartulovic

Interior Layout by Lori Michelle

Printed in the United States of America

First Edition

Visit us on the web at:
www.bloodboundbooks.net

Also from Blood Bound Books:

Out of suffering have emerged the strongest souls; the most massive characters are seared with scars.

~Khalil Gibran

PROLOGUE

PEST CONTROL TECHNICIANS have much in common with veterans; they wear their mental scars like medals and their self-worth is primarily encapsulated by the worst thing that ever happened to them. Most of them suffer from a muted sense of PTSD and they spend much of their idle time sharing war stories.

Call it a coping mechanism.

This is one of those stories about one of those men. This is a story about mental scars which run skin deep. This is a story about the Bug Man.

In Apartment 4 he began to understand, but in the beginning he was mostly untouched and completely oblivious.

ONE

LIMBO

*I postpone death by living, by suffering, by
error, by risking, by giving, by losing.*
~Anais Nin

Chapter One
Delusional Parasitosis

CLINT REACHED FOR the buzzer and the door to Apartment
4 flung open. A young woman with dark, frizzy hair
asked, "Are you here to spray?" There was a hint of
desperation in her tone.

"Yes, ma'am."

She sighed and said, "Thank God. It's about time."

Clint stepped into the narrow kitchen. The woman was
pale and thin with slender arms, long legs, and the neck of a
swan. She stared Clint in the eyes and her green irises were
fully circled by white with red veins scattered throughout.
She wore skintight black leggings, knee-high boots with fur
trim, and a long sleeved T-shirt with The Strokes printed
across her chest. Clint figured she was in her early to mid-
twenties, but she was so thin that her sexuality was lost—a
European fashion model slowly strolling down the catwalk,
then quickly ushered back into Auschwitz.

Clint looked away from her stare, which was so intense
that it seemed hysterical. "Have you seen any pests, ma'am?
Roaches? Ants?"

They Don't Check Out

"Both," she said and quickly added, "and gnats and flies and sometimes little spiders. And the bugs with lots of legs."

"Centipedes?"

"Yes, and I hear rats in the walls."

"Wow," Clint said. "Sounds like you've got a full scale infestation."

Clint surveyed the kitchen—it was as clean as a museum, floors polished and counters shiny. It smelled like a pine forest drenched with bleach. No sign of dishes and the sink sparkled. Clint shot several bursts of Deltamethrine around the baseboards and underneath a humming refrigerator that was adorned with several magnetic letters that formed the words: STAY FOCUSED. Clint opened the cabinet beneath the sink and saw a yellow bottle of Mr. Clean, a stack of multicolored sponges, and several Brillo pads. Not a roach in sight.

Clint could feel her watching him as he placed roach bait behind a blue bottle of Windex. He opened up two more cabinets that would traditionally hold pots and pans—they were empty.

The pantry was also empty except for a single shelf that held eight twelve-packs of Diet Coke and five boxes of saltine crackers. Clint sprayed the empty shelves and closed the door.

She was staring at him—eyes impossibly wide. Almost lidless.

"The poison is safe," Clint said.

"Why?" she asked. "I want this infestation gone. I don't care what it takes."

"It'll kill every insect," Clint said defensively. "It works on their nervous system. It's very effective. I just mean it's safe for you."

"Whatever it takes," she said. "I can't live like this anymore."

Clint stepped past her and moved into the living room. It was empty except for a glass coffee table and two red folding

4

chairs that looked more like lawn furniture. The walls were bare. The floors were clean enough to eat off of—though the options were limited to crackers and diet soda.

Clint walked around the room and sprayed the baseboards.

"Have you ever treated an infestation this severe?"

Clint looked up and she was staring at him, her eyes somehow wider.

Probing.

"Ma'am, I don't know what problem you used to have, but your apartment is cleaner than most hospitals."

"Don't you see them?" she asked indignantly.

"See what?"

"The bugs," she said.

Clint glanced around the sparse living room. "Where? Are you seeing them in the bathroom? Your bedroom?"

She stared at him, exasperation coloring her pale face. "How long have you been doing this?"

"For years," Clint said. "I'm a fully licensed technician. General pest. Lawn and ornamental. Termites—"

"Termites?" she shouted. "What do they look like?"

"Calm down. There's no way you've got them in here. There would be rotted wood or—"

"What do they look like?"

"They look a lot like flying ants. Their abdomens are—"

"I've seen them," she interrupted. "Thousands of them."

"Recently?"

"Very."

Clint walked past her and into the bathroom. It was pristine. A single white bar of soap, a green loofah, and a bottle of Herbal Essence shampoo. The medicine cabinet held an electric toothbrush, a tube of Crest Whitening toothpaste and three bottles of Pepto Bismol.

Clint looked up.

She was standing in the doorway.

"Well?" she asked.

"Believe me," Clint said. "There's no sign of anything."

"No sign of anything?" She laughed. "We make allowances for what we do not wish to see, don't we? I used to do the same. My family used to ask me, 'Where did you get those bruises from?' I told them, I don't know, I bruise easily. 'And your arm, how did you break it?' I fell. They suspected my first husband, Frank. And after he left me, they suspected my boyfriend, Byron. And then they suspected my second husband, Donald. 'Why do you keep choosing men who will hurt you?' I'm not. I was in a wreck. I was gang-raped by robbers. I think they were black, but they were wearing masks." She laughed and added, "I even told them I have a genetic disorder—brittle bone disease. I don't think they really believed me, but we make allowances for what we don't want to see."

"Well, there's nothing to see here."

"I know they are here," she insisted. "There are more of them at night. What do you call it?"

"Nocturnal?"

"Yes," she said. "I know they are here. You have to look harder."

Clint waited for her to step aside, but she continued to stand in the doorway. He took a step toward her and she didn't budge. "Do you want me to spray the bedroom?"

"Of course I do, Bug Man," she said. "That's where they are the worst."

She took a step back and he squeezed past her and stepped into her bedroom. The bed was made so tidily that it would have passed military inspection. There was a bottle of EZ-Sleep on her bedside table and a few brown prescription bottles. Clint glanced at them and she said, "I have to take my medicine every day."

Clint considered for a moment and asked, "What for?"

"My doctors say I have delusional parasitosis. I think it's ridiculous, but I humor them."

"I've never heard of it," Clint said. He opened her

closet. Her clothing was expertly hung on wooden hangers and several shoes were arranged on a hanging bamboo rack.

"It started when I realized some kind of bug crawled into my ear while I was asleep."

"What?" Clint turned and saw her standing only a few feet away from him.

She was holding a box cutter.

"They think I imagined it, but I know better."

Clint stared at the razor sharp edge of the blade. "Okay."

"It probably died in there years ago."

"Okay."

"But it laid eggs. Thousands of them."

Clint held the copper wand in front of him as if to ward her off—perhaps squirt her a few times if she got any closer with the blade.

"What's wrong?" she asked.

Clint took a step back, deeper into the closet. "What are you doing with that box cutter?"

"I'm going to show you; make you believe me. You say my bugs are nocturnal, but I'm going to wake them." She pulled up the sleeve of her T-shirt and revealed a fragile arm that was ravaged with deep horizontal scars; it looked like someone took her arm and forced it into a paper shredder.

Some of the wounds were fresh—a thin layer of scabbing just holding back a bloody torrent. She shifted the box-cutter into her left hand and let the blade hover just above her wounds.

"What did you do to yourself?" Clint asked.

"I tried to get them out of me," she shouted. "You can't comprehend how it feels. Something living inside of you and feeding off of you, bit by bit. Sometimes I can almost forget they're in me, but then the itching begins again and I can see them moving just beneath the skin."

"What do you see?"

"I've already told you. When it started it was only an itching that came from within my ear, like maybe a hair tickling my eardrum and only at night—right before sleep. At first I tried to ignore it and then I tried ear drops, like for swimmer's ear, and then ear candling, and then any kind of bullshit you could imagine.

"The itching only grew worse. Doctor Sokunbi told me it was all in my head—psychosomatic—but I knew better. Something crawled in my ear one night, most likely a cockroach, and laid eggs next to my brain."

Clint stared at the box cutter and slowly nodded.

"You'd think all of the baby cockroaches would want to come back out, but they don't. They've got plenty to eat in here." She gestured at her head with her empty hand. "You know we only use like fifteen percent of our brains, right? Probably, they just haven't gotten around to eating any of the important parts yet. Sometimes I forget things—basic stuff like eating or showering. Sometimes I just break into tears for no reason. It's the worms burrowing their way into me—deeper and deeper."

"Worms?"

"Yeah, I've got them in me as well. Maybe worms isn't the word for it—larvae. Like baby mosquitoes or flies. Only some of them are at least four inches long and they've got bristles on their legs. I can feel them slithering around inside of me like parasitic veins and arteries." She stared at her arm and added, "Did you see that? Must know I'm talking about them. One of them came right up to the surface of my skin, only careful not to poke out. I'd rip it out of me if it did, but they like to stay in me. As deep as possible."

"Ma'am, I think you are imagining it. Have you taken your medication today?"

She considered and said, "I'm not sure. I forget."

"I need to go."

"No," she screamed and she took a step toward him.

Clint took a step back and bumped into the rear wall.

"You have to cure my infestation," she screamed. "You have to do it, Bug Man. It's your job."

"No. You don't have any—"

"Yes, I do," she screamed and she brought the box cutter down to her forearm and cut into one of the fresh scabs. Blood flowed down her arm and dripped onto the wooden floor. "Do you see them?"

"There's nothing there," Clint mumbled. "Nothing."

"They're in there!" She dug the tip of the box cutter into a spot just beneath her palm and slowly drug it down her forearm until it reached her bicep. Her eyes grew wild.

"I have to go," Clint pleaded as he crouched down in the back of the closet. "Please let me out of here."

"Not until you've treated me," she screamed.

"There's nothing I can do."

She dropped the box cutter and ripped at the open gash in her arm, dug her fingers under the skin, and frantically peeled it back.

Clint looked away; he was certain he saw bone. Her dresses were neatly arranged on the hangers. The shoes hung compliantly on the bamboo rack. Clint stared at a pair of red Tom's with prints of black tigers and elephants.

"Look at them," she screamed.

Clint glanced up. Her forearm was a bloody mess and now she was peeling the skin away from her bicep. Her T-shirt was wet. Red poured out of her.

Clint aimed the bronze rod at her and held down the trigger. The Deltamethrine streamed out. She fell to her knees and closed her eyes and smiled. The poisonous stream washed down upon her like a cleansing rain. She was laughing as the persistent stream went into her mouth. A moment later she moaned and the sound was orgasmic.

Clint was gagging as he leapt over her and ran out of the bedroom.

There was movement all around the living room. Thousands of roaches scurried out from behind the molding that circled the ceiling and floor. Flies poured out of the air conditioning vent.

Clint ran into the kitchen and saw an angry mass of insects streaming out of the faucet. The ceiling throbbed above him and several wood roaches fell from the ceiling, landed on Clint's head, and ran across his face.

Back in the bedroom he could hear her laughing.

He opened the door and stumbled out of the kitchen and slammed it behind him. He quickly patted himself down and searched for intruders.

Nothing.

He dug a pinkie into each of his ears and tried to shake it out, but somewhere within he could still hear her laughing.

Only then did he realize he didn't ask her for a key to the lobby door.

He was still trapped.

Chapter Two
Sexual Cannibalism

SEXUAL CANNIBALISM IS when a female kills and consumes her male counterpart before, during, or after copulation. Though this act is rare within the animal kingdom, it most often occurs among spiders or scorpions. Females may cannibalize unwanted males as a method of mate rejection or use cannibalism to regulate the timing of copulation. The removal of the head of some insects causes ejaculation to occur quicker.

Direct mate choice via sexual cannibalism is a result of a specific discrimination by females, often by size, since size is strongly correlated with a variety of fitness characteristics.

Being eaten also benefits the male since he serves as a kind of vitamin for his offspring so that they are strong enough to survive. And he gets to pass on his genes. The fact of the matter is that sexual cannibalism isn't that uncommon in nature. Especially in the insect world, male redback and orbweb spiders fall prey to their lovers, not to mention the infamous black widow.

Chapter Three
Prepare for the Worst

CLINT STERN STARED at Mr. Carrion; his boss stood behind a podium covered with a poster showcasing a mass of pale, blind subterranean termites feeding on some oblivious asshole's structural timbers within the walls of his cozy decaying domicile. Mr. Carrion stared out at his army of pest control technicians, smiled, and shouted, "Business is booming gentlemen."

Mr. Carrion was the proud owner of Southeastern Pest Control, and he spent three decades building it, starting in San Augustine in 1978 as a one-man business. He then expanded to Hemphill, Jasper, Lufkin, and finally established the home office in Nacogdoches, the oldest town in Texas. He defined himself as the godfather of pest control for East Texas, and Orkin and Terminex could eat his shit. He was once a handsome man with wiry muscles and thick blond hair, but time and prosperity erased these qualities and he became soft and wrinkled with thin gray hair that receded below the top of his ears, and these he combed up from the back and over his bald head in a futile attempt to offer the illusion of youth. He wore a navy blue jumpsuit every day and let the zipper dangle too low, revealing a fragile chest covered with gray hairs that resembled a pubic thatch.

Mr. Carrion's path to success was legendary. In the early years, he attended a conference for small business owners and he was told that as the head of a small business, his values bleed into the company culture whether intentional or not. That stuck with him and he decided to build a business philosophy for Southeastern Pest Control that would separate him from his competitors. It wasn't "the customer is always right" or "go above and beyond service" or the sickeningly ambiguous "never stop improving." Corporal Elton Carrion fought in Vietnam and many of his actions might have been mislabeled as wartime atrocities by pussy liberals but, in his mind, they were just good business. With this knowledge in mind, his business motto was "scare the customer badly enough and they will pay whatever it takes."

The culmination of this concept was a pamphlet about potential pests he left with every new customer that was simply titled: *Fun Facts*. He meticulously gathered the information and wrote eye-catching headlines including: "Little Vampires," "Dying on Your Back," and his personal favorite, "Sexual Cannibalism." He even included a few vivid photos, such as a brown recluse bite that had rotted away a softball-sized hole in a man's leg and left the tendons and bone exposed. He believed that fear was the greatest motivator, and to prove his point, his customer retention was unparalleled.

Mr. Carrion instilled this philosophy in his employees and he ran his business like a finely tuned military unit. He stared out at his soldiers and continued, "Last week the lead story on KTRE news was about a seven-year-old boy in Angelina County who was taken to the emergency room with a cockroach in his ear after the school nurse called the authorities. Turns out the kid's parents are a couple of meth addicts. The kid reeked of cat urine and had worn the same pull-ups to school two weeks in a row, and the teachers were bathing and cleaning him. Blah, blah, blah. The important part—and what people will remember—is that glorious little bastard of a roach squealing in his ear. Our phone has been ringing off the hook with new clients and you better believe I'm updating the Fun Facts pamphlet.

"What that means for y'all is plenty of overtime. So, even though I'm sure y'all are excited it's Friday, I would suggest you don't make any weekend plans."

Clint and his fellow pest control technicians stifled their groans of complaint, well aware that it would be interpreted as disloyalty and Mr. Carrion was known to fire staff on the spot to prove a point.

Mr. Carrion continued, "In addition to your expanding routes, there are a few more orders of business. Mike Moses Middle School has a pressing issue. The science teacher, Ms. Woods, purchased three black gerbils that promptly bit her and then chewed through their plastic home that night. The principle was understandably concerned; however, I assured him domesticated gerbils carry no threat of rabies." Mr. Carrion paused, winked, and added, "Unless, of course, they are running wild and are bitten by a rabid animal. Of greater concern is that they have left behind a trail of scat and destruction—they chewed up three rugs and a bean bag. The custodians can't seem to find them and the teachers are squeamish."

Hollis Barber leaned in toward Clint. "Why's it always got to be black gerbils?"

Clint shrugged and whispered, "I think you mean African-American gerbils."

"Why do I get the feeling when you say 'African-American,' what you really mean is 'nigger'?"

"True," Clint agreed. "But when I say 'nigger,' I mean 'African-American'."

Hollis smiled and mumbled, "First place I'd check for those gerbils is up Mr. Carrion's asshole."

Mr. Carrion cleared his throat and said, "Mr. Barber, did you have an opinion you wanted to share with us?"

"No, sir," Hollis said.

"Good. I'm going to let you handle this, along with your usual route; wait until after five when the students are well gone. I suggest you hit every room with rat traps, and you might as well use some mice poison as well. I figure gerbils fall somewhere within that spectrum. Make damn sure you place the baits in spots where the students can't get to it. Last thing we need is a lawsuit because one of those assholes tries to get high snorting Brodifacoum. F-Y-I, we are charging the school double."

"Okay," Hollis said.

"Now, for some even bigger news," Mr. Carrion said. "I'm pleased to announce that Southeastern Pest Control has acquired an important new client. More specifically, I recently negotiated an exclusive contract with Farmbridge Development, a company that specializes in purchasing tracts of undeveloped land and setting up subdivisions filled with cookie-cutter houses; however, upon occasion they also renovate existing structures and establish low-income housing."

"Roach motels," Hollis muttered.

Clint nodded in agreement. He had been around long enough to know that low income was a nice way of saying government housing for society's bottom feeders, and he treated enough HUD hellholes to know their tenants lived in squalor sufficient to embarrass a potbellied pig.

Mr. Carrion noted the judgmental stares of his technicians and he raised his hands defensively and said, "If you want to date the prom queen you have to get her chubby sister laid."

"Shit," Hollis said. "I'll fuck the prom queen *and* her chubby sister. In fact, throw her fat ass momma up in it too."

Mr. Carrion frowned and asked, "Mr. Barber, have you received a single raise since you've been with us?"

"No, sir."

"As I was saying," Mr. Carrion continued, "there are a number of buildings which I would have to classify as less than stellar that nonetheless need our immediate attention. In addition to your routes, several of you will also be treating one of these buildings. My suggestion is that you take more chemical than you think is necessary. Prepare for the worst, but expect even worse."

Clint cranked his red Ford F-150 and stared at his work order; along with his usual route of sixteen houses, he had been given a dump called Mystic Valley Housing located on 1620 Martin Luther King Drive. He watched as Hollis approached his truck, lowered his window and asked, "Are you okay, man?"

Clint realized something in his expression was a bit off—his eyes too wide and his lips too thin. Typically Hollis was a lighthearted man who was almost sickeningly positive, but now he was shaken.

"I need to switch assignments, bro. Not the whole thing, but for sure the new one." He handed Clint a card with the name and address of his new assignment courtesy of Farmbridge Development. "Carrion is trying to fuck me. I know it."

Clint read the card. "Hampton Place Living Facilities? Hollis, it doesn't sound that bad. Why are you so worked up?"

"Hampton Place is what it's called now, but the address . . ." Hollis swallowed and asked, "Don't you know what the place used to be?"

Clint glanced at the card again. "No. It's out of town a ways I think, but I don't remember driving down Sunny Brook Lane."

Hollis frowned and said, "That spot used to be a nuthouse. My momma's uncle spent some time in the place back in the day. I just don't think I can go there." He reached through the window, squeezed Clint's shoulder. "Can you help me?" he asked.

"I'd like to, man, but Jenn is going to be livid as it is. She's been coming down on me already for working too much and now she's on bed rest."

"What is she, seven months pregnant?"

"Eight, and she's on the verge of preeclampsia."

"What's that?"

"Basically it's high blood pressure. She's tired all the time and her feet swell up, and if it gets any worse it can be dangerous for her. Not that it's your problem, man, but I'm already on thin ice. I've been drinking too much and just last night I promised her I'd get my shit together."

"Bro, what if I pick up some of your route? That way you don't get in trouble with your woman and I don't have to go to a place where my uncle was given daily treatments of shock therapy."

Clint stared down at his wedding ring. It was black and made of tungsten, supposed to be damn near unbreakable, but recently it began to crack. He glanced up at Hollis and said, "The new gig Carrion gave me is an apartment complex on MLK."

Hollis smiled and said, "Hell, bro, that's in the 'hood. That's my people. No one as white as you needs to go in there without a bodyguard."

"Take that and my three houses on Main Street and we have a deal."

"Hell, bro, I'll throw in a blow job as well. You the man."

Clint smiled. "No thanks. I owe you regardless; you always cover for me on termite inspections knowing I'm too fucking claustrophobic to crawl under a house. Switching gigs is the least I can do for you."

"You give Jenn a kiss for me, Clint, and when your son is born you can name him Hollis."

Clint rolled up his window and watched Hollis walk away and imagined his son comfortably curled within his wife's belly. A fragile nameless human floating in a dark limbo, void of expectations, utterly content and untarnished. Connected to his wife by an umbilical cord and she to him. She would be lying in bed watching some housewives show on Bravo while she anticipated each kick, their heartbeats synchronized. Meanwhile, Clint would be killing pests and anticipating the future while feeling distant and utterly alone.

Chapter Four
Abandon Hope

CLINT TYPED HAMPTON Place Living Facilities into Google Maps and realized it was almost thirty miles outside of town. That was going to set him back an hour he hadn't anticipated, and he was already running late.

The sun was betraying him again, only a bloody residue still visible and quickly fading. Ms. Clevenger walked him from one insignificant fire ant mound to the next over her four acres of cow pasture while a hostile and unforgiving noon-day sun hovered above. Afterward, the ungrateful bitch had the audacity to try to haggle down the bill.

After that he showed up late at a Tex-Mex shithole called Big Burrito that was owned by a bitter old Greek man who tried to adapt his former restaurant—Zorba's—after it failed to generate excitement over his gyros, dahmas, and hummus. He insisted on creating a rustic Texas appearance in his restaurant, as if butchering two cultures wasn't bad enough, so the joint was adorned with deer heads and the restaurant floor was covered with four inches of saw dust. What that meant was the bastard hadn't mopped his floors in over a year, yet he was perplexed and indignant that he had persistent, fly, roach, and rat infestations.

Every stop on the route was similarly frustrating and now the sky smoldered like a dying campfire and dark clouds threatened to hide the moon and stars.

What had he told Jenn, seventh-thirty at the latest? Now

almost six and he had an entire complex left to spray. To make matters worse, it was, as Carrion described it, a structure renovated for low-income housing. People who lived in HUD housing weren't known for their good hygiene, and in all likelihood, the last time the place had been sprayed was when Clint was still shitting his diapers.

The iPhone directed him down CR 214 and, according to the map, Hampton Place was located at the very end of the road. Clint hated to drive during dusk; his eyes had begun to show wear and in the meager light he was practically blind. He turned forty just two months prior and he figured it was mid-life and the trip went downhill from there. Gray hairs suddenly sprouted at his temples and a wave of them had formed in his goatee. His eyelids had begun to sag and he could barely get a hard-on anymore. Of course, that wasn't age. Just fear. Afraid to put his weight on his pregnant wife; he gained at least as many pounds as she had and most of it in his belly as well. Afraid he'd poke the baby and when he confessed as much to her, she laughed and he took it as an insult, wondering if she thought his dick was too small. Still, he feared hurting the baby, that lima bean they spotted on the ultrasound and watched grow each month when, six months into the pregnancy, they saw a penis that Clint could barely make out.

Like father, like son.

He texted Jenn: Running late, honey. Sorry.

He waited for her response and felt the pine trees closing in on either side of him. He flipped on his headlights as the sun hid somewhere behind him, and damn if he could see more than shadows in front of him.

The nurse practitioner had asked, "Do you want to know the sex of the baby?"

He felt a weight on his chest like he was sealed within a cement coffin falling into the depths of the ocean. True fear. He wanted to say, "No, let it be a surprise."

But Jenn had squeezed his hand and said, "Yes, we do."

"It's a boy."

Sinking to the ocean floor and him stuck inside with no air to breathe.

He smiled then and squeezed her hand back and imagined sharks circling all around and infinite darkness. A son. He was going to be a father. And he promised himself for the thousandth time that he wouldn't be like his father.

History doesn't always have to repeat itself.

Cycles can be broken.

His phone vibrated and he glanced at her text: Okay.

It might have seemed like an ambiguous response, but he knew her and when she said "okay" it signified disappointment, resentment, and resignation.

He quickly typed "I love you," but he drove into a dead spot and the phone was out of service.

Clint shoved the phone into the middle console, dug under a pile of receipts, and pulled out a pack of Marlboros. He promised Jenn he'd quit smoking. It was bad for her and worse for their unborn son. He sprayed himself down with Febreeze before he got home and made a beeline for the shower, telling her that he had to clean the pest control chemicals off of him. Tell her he had to wash it out of his clothing because they arc dangerous and he was exposed to them all day.

She would look at him knowingly and say, "Okay."

Up ahead he could see a white truck parked in the ditch and several orange pylons were set up in front of the mouth of a narrow bridge. A tall Hispanic man was waving a yellow flag that glowed in the growing darkness.

Clint slowed to a crawl and stopped a few feet in front of the bridge. A wide river ran through the woods and cut a deep ditch in the countryside; the bridge was the only way over the river. Clint rolled down his window and lit a cigarette. He sucked it down into his lungs, and for the first time in as long as he could remember, he became aware of his breathing. He took a long drag and watched the tip burn. Time seemed to stand still.

He realized he closed his eyes and when he opened them a Hispanic man was standing next to his window with a cloud of smoke encircling his head. The Hispanic man wore a bright orange vest and a hard hat and a name tag across his narrow chest that read: Charro.

He was the oldest Mexican Clint had ever seen, at least in his nineties, with sunken cheeks and a road map of time etched into his forehead. His right eye was a fierce blue that belonged on a much younger man and his left eye was lifeless, the pupil covered by a thick white membrane.

Clint cleared his throat and asked, "Is the road closed?"

The ancient Mexican shook his head. "You have to pay to go across."

Clint almost laughed, but the dead eye was fixed on him and the Mexican's expression remained humorless. It was a shakedown. Clint briefly considered plowing through the pylons and giving the old man the finger as a proper *adios*, but he'd been brought up to respect the elderly. He reached into his billfold and pulled out a five dollar bill and asked, "How's that?"

The Mexican snatched it out of his hand and slowly walked away and gathered his orange pylons and stacked them in the back of his truck. Clint figured it was a scam he ran at the end of his shift and the illicit toll was most likely going toward a bottle of Kentucky Hunter. Ah, well, let the old fucker have it. God bless him.

Clint eased across the bridge and the wooden planks groaned beneath him. On the other side of the bridge the paved road morphed into red dirt that was as bright and wet as a fresh wound. The road wound through dense piney woods for about a half mile, and then the trees parted and revealed a monstrous building made of sullen gray stone. Clint counted the rows of orderly windows that stretched up the surface of the obscene structure and realized it was five stories high, not including a windowless attic. Twenty windows across each story and he could only see the front.

The sides stretched back and were lost in darkness. There could be hundreds of apartments in the dump. He wasn't prepared for a job like this. No fucking way. It could take days to spray it. Hell, a lifetime. Carrion must have been trying to make a point to Hollis, maybe make him quit.

Clint considered turning around and driving home to Jenn. He could drive through Peking, surprise her with General Tso's chicken and fried rice, and serve it to her in bed. After gorging themselves, they'd open fortune cookies and he'd tell her his reading: The future has never been brighter. He would lean in and place a soft hand on her belly and gently kiss her lips. He would hold her the way he used to before she had purchased the full body pillow and slept with it between them—a nightly reminder of how distant they had become.

Clint pulled into a dimly lit parking lot and killed the engine. Carrion would fire Hollis over this, no doubt. That would suck, but what if Hollis told Carrion that they traded gigs? Would Carrion fire Clint as well? He might. He probably would.

Clint lit another cigarette and tried to imagine a scenario that didn't end with him on unemployment and Jenn staring at him vacantly and whispering "okay."

He surveyed the parking lot and realized there were only six other vehicles: three cars, two trucks, and a van parked in a handicapped spot in front of the entrance. Unless there was additional parking somewhere in the back of the building, most of the complex was unoccupied. Maybe they were still in the process of renovating the structure one section at a time or maybe there were only a handful of people willing to live out in the sticks.

Clint inhaled deeply and felt anxiety gather in his lungs and then he blew it out in a cloud of smoke. That had to be it—they were probably renovating the place one section at a time and there were less than a dozen unlucky souls living in there. He'd go in and give it the old in and out and then haul ass home.

They Don't Check Out

He walked to the bed of his truck and sprung the lock on a large black toolbox. He pulled out a backpack sprayer that held six gallons that had already been mixed with the maximum amount of Deltamethrin legally allowed. He pulled it onto his back, the weight of it was comforting and balanced him. After a full day's work it took him several hours to adjust to the loss of weight. Clint wondered if Jenn would experience a similar sensation once the baby was born.

Clint loaded a bait gun with a fresh gel tube of roach poison and grabbed a plastic bag filled with roach baits and another filled with ant baits and an assortment of anti-vermin paraphernalia that included rat poison and glue traps. Clint placed these items in a satchel he wore on his hip that looked a lot like a large fanny pack, but wasn't nearly as faggy because what it held inside was death.

A dense fog slowly drifted in and Clint wondered if that river ran down to a larger body of water somewhere near. Clint approached the vile structure. Up close it reminded him a bit of the dormitory he had spent his first three semesters of college in and a lot of the funeral home he had gone to when he was seven. His mother had been pale and waxy, her face set in a frown and her arms lay across her chest. He cried when his father told him to go say good-bye to her, and when he refused his father dug his boney fingers into Clint's hips and pushed him all the way up to the coffin.

Her eyes were closed. She wore a dress that reminded him of their last day together. She had taken them to Pecan Park to feed old bread to the ducks.

Clint forced the ghosts of the past away and noticed a Trojan wrapper that had been tossed onto one of the steps that led to the entrance. Within the decaying walls a network of cracks spread like spider veins in an obese woman's pale thighs. He glanced up and could only see three stories high. The rest was lost in the heavy night. The windows were barred and covered with dark blinds that dispelled the weak light from the surrounding street lamps.

Clint moved toward the entrance and each step was forced, as if his father was once again pushing him forward.

The double doors at the entrance were made of thick unfriendly iron; likely a throwback to the times when it had been an asylum and their primary function was to keep inmates in rather than welcome visitors. Clint grabbed the doorknob and held a small hope that it would be locked, but the door easily swung open.

TWO

LUST

We are never so defenseless against suffering as when we love.

~Sigmund Freud

Chapter Five
Apart Anger

HE DOOR OPENED up to a wide lobby. The floors were smooth and made of obsidian though, obviously, they couldn't be. Jenn wanted a kitchen counter made of the stuff and the cost had been prohibitive. Florescent bulbs flickered above and emitted a sickly blue-tinted glow like a bug zapper. The lobby was strangely inviting, a stark contradiction to the unwelcoming entrance.

Clint walked to the glass lobby door and noticed that some smart-ass had scratched away a few of the stenciled red letters and changed the wording from "Apartment Manager" to "Apart Anger." The hours below read "M-F 8:00-7:00" in small print. According to a round clock mounted above the door it was almost 7:00. Good. He'd tell the manager that he needed to reschedule for next week and Hollis could come back and spray the dump himself.

He turned the knob. Locked.

He put his ear to the door and could hear a radio within playing "Ice, Ice, Baby." He rapped on the frame, one time gently and then three times with force.

The handle turned and the door flew open.

"The office is closed!"

"I'm with Southeastern Pest Control," Clint said.

"Ahhh, the Bug Man."

A figure emerged from the office and Clint froze, then quickly stared down at his feet and tried not to emote the repulsion that struck him as suddenly as if he stepped into a steaming pile of dog shit barefoot. He dared another glance at the monstrosity who stood in front of him. *Good, God.* Clint looked away again and pretended to search for a business card, fully aware he kept them in his shirt pocket.

"Running late, aren't you?" He spoke with a lisp and his tone was high pitched and effeminate. Clint immediately wondered if he was gay.

Clint forced a polite smile and reached into his front pocket and withdrew a business card and extended it to the apartment manager. The man's mouth was horribly malformed and Clint figured he was born with a horrendous hair-lip, but it looked like it had been haphazardly sewn together with shoelaces. "Clint Stern, nice to meet you."

He snatched the card and said, "Earl Guin." He couldn't have been an inch over five feet, but he managed to pile over four hundred pounds on his small frame. His squished face sat on folds of skin so thick that it looked like a fleshy neck brace. His beady eyes were mostly lost under droopy eyelids, like a Shar Pei puppy, and his malformed upper lip revealed a mouthful of teeth as tiny and yellow as corn kernels. His short blond hair was as soft and thin as the feathers on a baby duck. He embraced his obesity because he was wearing an Under Armor shirt that would have been tight on a heroin addict. The cloth squeezed him tighter than a medieval corset or a straightjacket.

Clint had an aunt who was anorexic so he was well aware of the concept of body dysmorphia, but this guy seemed to have it in reverse. Maybe, when he looked into the mirror what he saw was Johnny Depp staring back at him.

All of that was troubling, but the part that really got to Clint was that Earl stood on a single leg; his other limb ended just above the knee and his denim pant leg had been pinned under, covering the stump.

Earl must have read his revulsion because he defensively said, "The doctor told me I had no choice but to lose it. Says I'm diabetic. Well, I was diabetic. I've been dieting. Fruits and veggies."

Clint nodded and wondered if a Twinkie was classified as a fruit or a vegetable. "I'm sorry for my tardiness; it has been a crazy day."

"I bet." He turned and hopped back into the office. Clint stared wide-eyed and thought of a bloated tick he once burned off his dog. It held firmly as the match burned into its stretched skin and then burst with a pop, leaving only a bloody blot to mark its passing.

Clint followed him into the office and wondered if Earl's remaining leg would eventually splinter beneath the awful burden it was forced to carry.

"Listen," Clint said. "I know it's late so I'm happy to reschedule you for first thing next week."

Earl frowned and said, "Unacceptable. Management will not be pleased. Mr. Carrion assured me the building would be treated today. I was adamant about this. The infestation has become intolerable. Besides, I have already put out the Prior Notice forms, the tenants are expecting you."

"I hear you," Clint said, "but it's late. I don't mind—"

"I'll just call Mr. Carrion now," Earl interrupted, his voice slightly less masculine than Clint's hairstylist. He picked up a phone receiver and glanced at the business card and frantically struck the buttons with his fat fingers.

"No need," Clint said. "I can do it now."

Earl giggled and gently hung up the phone. He took three hops over to a closet door, opened it, and dug around inside.

Clint took a deep breath, realizing how close he had come to being terminated. He decided to smooth the waters so he said, "Interesting job you got here, managing apartments and such."

"Tedious and boring," he replied. Keys rattled in the closet and when Earl hopped back out he was holding a large key ring filled with numbered keys. He handed it over and Clint was relieved to note that his earlier assumption about the occupancy rate was fairly accurate—only a few dozen keys. "We only have twenty units at this point, but occupancy is increasing as quickly as the rooms can be renovated. I won't trouble you to spray the empty apartments. There are hundreds of them."

Clint smiled and nodded.

"I assured Mr. Carrion that this will eventually be a very lucrative contract. He was excited."

"I bet," Clint agreed.

"So far Management has been renovating apartments which are of an appropriate size and in the least ill repair. As it happens, there are four occupied apartments on each floor. I live in Apartment 5 on the second floor. The stairs are unfortunate, but I felt it had the best window view. There is a pond with ducks."

Clint nodded and asked, "When was the last time a pest company treated these premises?"

"As far as I know it's been many years. Certainly not since it's been reopened. I've been told the entire asylum, inside and out, used to be treated with a liberal dosage of Diazinon."

Clint laughed, "I'm sure that did the trick."

"I understand that the product has since been deemed unsafe."

"Absolutely," Clint agreed. "Diazinon is an organophosphate."

"Meaning?"

"Well, it's not all that different than the nerve gas used during World War II. It certainly killed pests, but it wasn't so healthy for humans either. The EPA discovered that even short-term exposure caused headaches, nausea, or dizziness and long-term exposure could cause seizures, paralysis, mental disorders, comas, and sometimes it was fatal. In particular, children are susceptible to it."

"Sounds like rubbish," Earl said. "Political propaganda made up by some lobbyists' interest hired by a pest control company intent on taking the power out of the hands of the consumer. No matter, you got your way; Carrion is charging us an arm and a leg."

"Actually, *we* can't even use it anymore," Clint said.

"A pity. I do hope your current means are effective?"

"No doubt," Clint said. "And much safer for your tenants as well."

Earl smiled, but his misshapen lip turned it into a sneer. "This way," Earl said and he hopped past Clint and led him down the hallway. Clint trailed at a safe distance in case the lone leg finally decided to give up the ghost.

The hallway ended in front of a winding set of stairs. The first floor branched out to the left and right, and the hallway was equal distance on both sides. The stairs appeared to have been recently carpeted an unsightly Pepto Bismol pink. "Apartments one and two are to our left and three and four are located to our right. This pattern repeats itself all the way up to the attic. As you see, there are dozens of doors on each side that are locked and truth be told there's no telling what horrors hide behind them. I'm certain most of them are in a state of disrepair. Be grateful Management doesn't want you to treat them as well."

"Thanks."

"I was told Farmbridge briefly considered just tearing the whole structure down and starting anew. Thankfully they reconsidered."

"I heard this used to be an asylum."

"Ah, yes. You are correct. Fascinating, really." Earl sat down on the pink stairs and gently patted the space next to him.

Clint pretended not to notice the invitation and remained

standing a fair distance away. He cursed himself for mentioning the asylum, realizing Earl was gearing up to give him a history lesson while Jenn was waiting for him at home silently counting the ways he had let her down, the list growing by the minute.

"As you are probably aware," Earl began, "this facility is perhaps most notoriously known as the Piney Woods Asylum for the Criminally Insane, but that wasn't always the case. I did a little research and found out that back in 1914 it was called the Melrose State Hospital for the Negro Insane."

"A more politically correct name I've never heard," Clint said. "The only difference in the newer incarnation was they changed the word Negro to Criminal. Good ole East Texas."

Earl laughed and said, "You can't blame southern prejudice for such a label. Have you ever heard of Benjamin Rush?"

"I don't think so," Clint admitted, wondering if there was a graceful way to avoid what sounded like a rehearsed monologue.

"He's known as the Father of American Psychiatry, and among his vast credentials, he was a signer of the Declaration of Independence and the Dean of the Medical School for the University of Pennsylvania. His portrait still adorns the official seal of the American Psychiatric Association. Mr. Benjamin Rush, MD once declared, in an official capacity, no less, that Negroes all suffer from an affliction called Negritude. He considered it to be a mild form of leprosy."

"You're shitting me!" Clint said.

"No, not at all. Look it up if you don't believe me. And that isn't even the best part. Do you know what the respected Dr. Rush prescribed as the only cure for the dreaded affliction of Negritude?"

"Shit, man, I don't know. Watermelon and collard greens?" Earl exploded into laughter and Clint turned away until his fat had settled into place. "Sorry about that. It was an off-color remark. Not really appropriate."

"No, no, very appropriate. You just don't know. At least your solution is attainable. Mr. Rush stated the only cure for the dreaded Negritude was to become white. Now, I wonder how many of his patients were successfully cured?"

"Not many, I don't guess."

"Quite right. Not many at all. Now, as I was saying before skipping off on such a delightful tangent, the Melrose State Hospital for the Negro Insane was opened in 1914 and, true to its name, any blacks in the area labeled as insane were forcibly admitted. During those times insanity and retardation or even physical handicaps were often interchangeable. Back then there were four other buildings at least as large as this one that have since been condemned, bulldozed, and carted away in manageable pieces. All that remains is this building, the farm, and a small graveyard serving as the final resting place for the former inmates. I once heard from an educated man that back in the Civil War days there was a fair amount of low-grade iron deposits in the area buried beneath the layers of red clay. In addition, he said they mined deposits of coal for the furnaces. I don't know if it's true, but just west of the graveyard is a small field which constantly emits smoke, almost as if there's a fire burning just beneath the top layer of earth. I was told by a janitor he'd dreamed it was an Indian burial ground."

"I think I saw that on the movie *Poltergeist*," Clint said. "Sounds like he fell asleep during a horror movie marathon."

"Perhaps," Earl admitted. "I do know the five buildings were laid out in such a way that if you drew lines and connected them it would form a pentagram."

"Strange."

"Yes, it is. Some places just have energy attached to them. I don't really know how to explain it, but I can undeniably say such is the case here. Initially, this facility housed only the mentally ill; however, beginning in 1952 Huntsville Penitentiary was kind enough to hand off their worst offenders and this very building served as a maximum security unit for the criminally insane. On the bright side, it was integrated, making no distinction between race or creed, only allowing they were suitably dangerous and deranged."

"Progress is beautiful."

"That it is. In the late seventies it became the Piney Woods Behavioral Health Center and remained such until President Reagan diligently began to work on budget savings and eventually the institution was closed. Most of the inmates were simply released on the streets; however, one by one most of the former patients found their way back. Apparently they were all turned away. Disheartening really. After a time Farmbridge purchased the facility and now I'm back."

"Back?"

"Did I mention I used to be an inmate? I'm better now . . . cured even. Hard to say the rest of the tenants are much of an improvement though. Most of them have little regard for their lodgings and, as is usually the case with something freely given, they do not value it."

"You mean because this is HUD?" Clint asked.

"Yes. Farmbridge has a government contract paying them $500 a month for each occupied unit, but the tenants pay nothing. Unfortunately, very few welfare recipients are willing to drive out this far even for free lodging."

"It is a bit of a trek," Clint said.

"That it is. Now I also know a bit about the asylum as it existed before it became a haven for the Negro insane. In the late 1800s it was allegedly a children's asylum. An orphanage, really. Word has it they were treated even more poorly than the negros, but who really knows the truth? Oh, well, the time grows late. Any further questions?" He braced himself against the wall and stood.

"No, I think you covered it. A pleasure meeting you."

Earl offered the semblance of a smile and extended a pudgy mitt.

Clint turned and pretended to sneeze. Without another

word, Earl hopped down the hallway and disappeared inside the office of the Apart Anger.

Chapter Six
Pathenogenesis

FEMALE COCKROACHES PREFER males at the bottom of the social order, but dominant males will attempt to rape them. In instances where females mate with low ranking males they produce fewer sons. In instances where no males are present females can reproduce without them through a process known as parthenogenesis; these offspring can only be female.

Some female cockroaches mate once and are pregnant for the rest of their lives. The male cockroaches transfer sperm to females in a package called a spermatosphere. Oftentimes, the males cover this package in a rich wrapping that the female can eat to obtain nutrients to raise her young.

CLINT MOVED DOWN the left-hand hallway and passed several doors that were as lonely and ambiguous as unmarked graves, until he stopped at a doorway marked with a metallic 1. He pressed a small button embedded in the frame, but he couldn't hear the doorbell ringing within. He rapped on the door and waited, but there was no answer. Clint inserted the appropriate key and let himself in.

The room was dark and he fumbled around and found a light switch. He stood in a narrow kitchen. The sink was filled with dirty dishes and a small stove-top held a pot half filled with dried up macaroni and cheese.

Clint yelled, "Hello? Pest control here."

Silence.

He opened a cabinet under the sink, withdrew his bait gun and applied a thin white line of poisonous gel in the furthest corner just behind an even more toxic yellow bottle of Mr. Clean. He repeated the procedure in a cabinet crowded with Tupperware and mismatched dishes and then again in a small pantry. In the crack between the refrigerator and the wall Clint inserted a round roach-bait covered in red plastic. It would attract a roach quicker than Earl to an all-you can-eat buffet. Clint had learned roaches are primarily attracted to four things: food, warmth, darkness, and vibrations; therefore, it was a given that he would need to treat within the cabinets and behind any large household appliances.

Clint stepped out of the kitchen and flipped another light switch that revealed a small living room/dining room combo. The walls had recently been painted eggshell white, but everything else in the apartment was old and worn down. Clint took the tank off his back, gave it a few pumps to prime up the fluid and strapped it back over his shoulders. He walked the perimeter of the room and sprayed the baseboards and the barred windows facing the parking lot.

A dead bonsai tree sat in the windowsill. A tiny statue of an old man sat at its roots and offered the impression that the tree was life-sized and Clint was a modern day Gulliver invading a strange new world.

The cramped living room was filled with over a dozen potted plants and an L-shaped couch covered with tattered quilts. A baby monitor was mounted on the wall next to a small television. Clint walked down a shoulder-width hallway, squirting his poison at six-inch intervals. He stepped into a bathroom, flipped on the light, and realized he needed to take a shit.

He took off his backpack, wiped off the seat with a handful of toilet paper, pulled down his pants and sat down. A bloody maxi pad sat in a wastebasket next to the toilet. He looked away and pushed.

The front door opened.

Clint had no choice but to clench his cheeks and quickly pull up his pants.

A woman hollered from the kitchen, "Hello? Bug Man?"

"Yes, ma'am." He carefully shuffled into the living room and added, "I was just finishing up."

She was a middle-aged blonde with sunken cheeks, hollow eyes, and a face that seemed to have been prematurely worn down by a lifetime filled with cheap booze and cigarettes. Her long fingernails had been painted blue and her lipstick was thick red. Clint had once known a woman who could have been her doppelganger.

He was twenty-two and he and a group of friends had

gone into a strip club located between Houston and Galveston called The Bermuda Triangle. It was a cheap prefab building that had a BYOB policy. Clint had only gone because it was his friend Frank's bachelor party. They had brought in a cooler filled with Miller-Lite and two bottles of Jägermeister. He and Jenn had been dating for a few months and she asked him not to go, but he was bound by tradition and peer pressure.

The strippers were fully nude with shaven vaginas and preposterous breasts as realistic as water balloons with stretched areola and perpetually erect nipples. The women were as expressionless as mannequins, robotically shaking their asses and sliding down poles and one of them did a split and the men cheered, but Clint felt ill.

They shotgunned a beer and a shot of Jägermeister after each dance.

Clint was critically aware that his penis remained flaccid in his pants, and as the night drew on he became sullen and distant. He refused all offers of a private dance, and by the end of the night he had positioned himself so that he was facing the exit.

Clint left alone and as he drove toward his hotel he realized he was so drunk that the road blurred beneath him. He pulled into a truck stop diner just outside Houston and decided to drink as much coffee and eat as many pancakes as it would take to sober him up. The waitress was named Gina and she was much older than him and she called him "honey" and laughed when he told her she was beautiful.

He asked her when she got off for the night and she blushed and walked away to get him a third stack of pancakes. He stared at her back and the gentle curve of her ass and he felt an unexpected stirring in his pants. Less than an hour later he followed her home.

She told him to be quiet as he stumbled into her house because her children were sleeping.

She wasn't beautiful at all, but when she reached into his

pants he almost exploded. The night was mostly a blur, but Clint remembered that as he ejaculated into her, he suddenly burst into tears. She held him and stroked his hair for several minutes as he sobbed.

He never told Jenn, but somehow he figured she knew and it was an unspoken secret between them which smoldered like an undying fire.

Clint stared more closely at the woman in front of him and realized she was much older than the truck stop waitress and even less attractive. She wore a tube top that emphasized her sagging breasts and a belly covered with deep stretch marks. Her denim miniskirt was too short for anyone who didn't spend their working hours on the street corner offering companionship by the half hour.

She smiled at Clint and said, "If I'd known you were coming I'd have cleaned up."

"No problem, ma'am."

She stared at Clint for a few seconds and said, "I'll be right back. I got to go outside and get Wayne Jr. and the rest of my groceries. Ain't safe to leave the door unlocked around here. You gonna be around for a few more minutes, sugar?"

Clint glanced over at the baby monitor and considered her question. She didn't think it was safe enough in the complex to leave the apartment unlocked, yet she had no problem leaving Wayne Jr. unattended outside? "Sure, ma'am. I'll hold the fort until you get back."

"Thanks, hon."

As soon as she left, Clint shuffled into the bathroom and finished what he started while he tried not to glance into the wastebasket. He stepped into a tiny bedroom and bumped into a cabinet filled with glassy-eyed porcelain dolls. The bed was covered with the lifeless children. Clint sprayed behind the bed and glanced at a vibrator that sat on the nightstand.

Clint was waiting in the hallway when the woman returned; she held a bag of potatoes in one hand and in her other she drug Wayne Jr. behind her on a leash. He was a nervous miniature Doberman Pinscher with a pair of testicles sufficient to shame a longhorn.

"Cute dog," Clint said.

"Only thing worth a damn I ever got out of Wayne Sr."

Clint wondered whether Wayne Sr. was a man or a full-sized Doberman and Wayne Jr. was a product of their forbidden lovemaking. A genetic anomaly created through bestiality, the stretch marks on her stomach a hint at the truth.

"Good night, ma'am."

She dropped the bag of potatoes on the counter and let the nervous dog off his leash. He scampered past Clint and into the bedroom. She raised a hand and asked, "Could I talk you into staying for dinner, Bug Man? It gets lonely here all by myself." Clint glanced at the baby monitor and she added, "Oh, goodness no. I'm as fertile as they come, but it always ends with a miscarriage."

"Always?" Clint mumbled.

"Sure. Over a dozen times so far."

"I'm sorry."

"Don't be. This world is no place to raise a child. They are far better off in heaven."

"Okay."

She smiled and said, "The last one was crying when I sucked her out. She couldn't have been more than two pounds, but Lord did she have a pair of lungs."

"Sucked her out?" Clint muttered as he shuffled past her and into the kitchen.

"Sure. It's called suction aspiration. I used to go into the clinic for it, but after a while they started eyeing me funny and asking judgmental questions. I ended up just getting my own vacuum. I keep it in the broom closet. You want to see it?"

"No."

"It's basically just a hollow tube with a knife-edged tip they shove up into your . . . Well, you know. It sucks harder than a two-dollar hooker." She laughed. "I'm so vulgar sometimes. You don't mind, do you?"

"I need to go."

"Please don't. Spend the night with me. I'm on the pill now."

"No." Clint shook his head. "I need to go spray the other apartments."

The baby monitor emitted a faint sound and Clint jumped.

She laughed and said, "That's just Wayne Jr., silly. My children don't cry. Not anymore. And you wouldn't hear them even if they could. I bury their little bodies in the flowerpots." She pointed at a pink Calla Lilly and said, "That's where I buried Cindy. You can't hear her no more."

Clint sprinted out of the kitchen and as he slammed the door her final words echoed, "It gets lonely."

Clint quickly moved down the hall with a mantra repeating in his mind: it gets lonely. He stopped in front of Apartment 2 and pressed the buzzer. He could hear it buzzing inside. Nobody home. It gets lonely. He used Earl's keys to open the door. The room was dark, but the light switch was in the same spot as the last room, and sure enough, he found he was standing within a narrow kitchen. There were no dirty plates in the sink or cleaning products stashed beneath it in the cabinet. There was no Uncle Ben's Rice in the cupboard or any other food for that matter. He flipped on the light in the living room. Empty. *Thank God*, he thought, *the apartment was vacant*. He decided to skip the gel and baits and just drench the place with spray before some strange soul came home and interrupted him. He walked along the perimeter of the kitchen and into the living room, spraying tight bursts of poison out of his copper rod.

It gets lonely.

The first bedroom was empty and the second one was similarly barren except for an old stained mattress lying against the back of the wall. The stain was shaped like a giant moth, but it was bloody and seemed to suggest lost virginity or some unknown violence. The florescent bulb flickered, playing a trick on Clint's eyes as it seemed like the bloody insect was fluttering its wings. Clint stepped closer and watched a drip from the ceiling fall and splash onto the stain. Clint looked up and saw a trickle of dirty water.

Or blood.

No, Clint thought, *not blood, just rusty water. Probably coming from a broken hot water heater in the unit above.*

Or a body.

Clint wasn't concerned. He'd check it out once he worked his way upstairs—or better yet, it was most likely one of the vacant rooms still in disrepair. Clint walked out of the room and just before he turned off the light the moth fluttered a final time and settled back into place.

Chapter Eight
Churning Curds

CLINT MOVED DOWN the hall and pressed the buzzer for Apartment 3. He could hear it buzzing inside. Nobody home. He helped himself inside with the appropriate key. The room was dark, but the light switch was still in the same spot, and of course he found himself standing within a narrow kitchen. A barren kitchen, for that matter. He flipped on the light in the living room.

Empty.

Good, he thought, *the apartment was as vacant as the last one.*

He could skip the gel and baits and just drench the place with Deltamethrine. He walked along the perimeter of the kitchen and into the living room, spraying tight bursts of poison out of his copper rod. He repeated the same process within both of the bedrooms and stepped into the bathroom.

He heard a steady trickle coming from the bathtub faucet, and behind a drawn white shower curtain adorned with lime green seahorses he could just make out a murky shadow.

"Is anyone there?"

"Bug Man?" came a faint whisper from behind the shower curtain.

"Yeah," Clint said. "Sorry, I thought this unit was unoccupied."

"That's an easy mistake." The voice was still soft and

fragile, but more substantial than the whisper. It was impossible to determine the gender of its source.

"Are you okay?" Clint asked.

"I've been better, but then again I try to see the bright side in any situation. Would you mind listening to me for a bit? I don't get much company."

The voice was so pitiful that Clint didn't have the heart to refuse. "Okay," he mumbled and he sat down on the edge of the toilet lid and tried to study the shadow behind the curtain. It was impossible to determine any sort of human form. The water continued to trickle steadily.

"You could say that I'm eternally optimistic and this skewed perspective has often led toward humiliating circumstances. Viewing a cup of piss as half full is one thing, but drinking it . . . I often misconstrued innocence as goodness, not remembering that man is born innocent, but like Lucifer before them the opportunity to discard such shackles abounds.

"I was in my late twenties, yet I'd only had sex with two women and with the first woman it was only once and for less than twenty frantic sloppy seconds that ended in regret and shame and a painful itch that persisted long afterward. I dated the second woman for three years and we were engaged for another and our sexual exploits were legendary— within my own mind at least.

"There was an instant chemistry between us and less than a year into the relationship we had methodically enacted every sexual position and intimate scenario within the *Joy of Sex* guidebook and moved on to the Kama Sutra. She was exceedingly flexible, being that she was a former gymnast, and we were able to bravely push our way through until we got to the standing positions. I am not a strong man, and the Tripod and most especially Churning Curds proved difficult. Regardless it was an intimate and pleasurable relationship during which we were both able to chalk up several notable references on our sexual résumés.

"One day she revealed she was a closet lesbian and that the past four years was a long sequence of tests I had failed. She was committed to remaining friends but really distant ones—more like illiterate pen pals. A week later I bumped into her in Kroger's holding hands with a woman who was much more masculine than I could ever hope to be. I went home and flipped through the *Joy of Sex* and cried myself to sleep.

"It was almost a year before I could even work up the nerve to ask another woman out on a date. She was a demure and unassuming secretary at my office who silently twisted her dark hair with one hand while she chewed the nails of her other. She chewed them down to nubs. She reeked of insecurity and in my indelible fashion I called it perfume. Angel. Obsession. Happy Heart.

"We went out to dinner at Johnny Carino's and walked through the Japanese gardens beneath a full moon and at the end of the night I reached down to kiss her and she recoiled. I asked her what was wrong and she mumbled, 'It's too soon. Far too soon.'

"I apologized and drove away, confused and disappointed. Regardless, I wasn't ready to give up on the blooming romance. On the third date she took my hand and on the fifth date she hugged me at the end of the night in front of her doorstep. I was tentative and submissive, should I accidentally violate some protocol I was unaware of. Despite my best attempts I occasionally erred. One night she caught me staring at her cleavage and demanded to be taken home. On another occasion my best friend made a crude joke about anal sex during a double date and I laughed too hard and too long for her liking.

"Though our upbringings and life experiences had been vastly different she expected me to strictly adhere to her moral code; however, she was so certain that her way was obvious and unerringly true that she refused to verbalize its intricacies. Therefore, I was left blind to stumble through a minefield of taboos. Her opinion was sacrosanct and should I cross it I would feel her silent wrath, and should I cross it too frequently she would have no recourse but to end the relationship.

"As a result, I began the relationship a fragile and disheartened man and gradually spiraled into an automaton of submissiveness; a dog that eagerly performed tricks with only a faint promise of reward. Until the sixteenth date. During a Disney double feature at the Cineplex she tapped me on the shoulder and whispered, 'Surprise me with a kiss at the end of the night.'

"I felt a flush that coursed through my cheeks and down into my pants, and as our fingers intertwined she watched the Little Mermaid swim to shore and magically sprout legs while I imagined more profane possibilities. Later, I walked her to the doorstep and pulled her in close and put my lips on hers and gently kissed her lower lip and then her upper. She grunted and opened her mouth and we bumped teeth. I giggled uncomfortably and she pulled me in close and bit my lip.

"I chalked the incident up to inexperience, but the next night she bit me hard enough to draw blood and the following night she put a grotesque hickey on my neck. I wondered if I'd unleashed a beast. One night while she was nibbling on my ear I bravely slid my hand under her blouse and let my fingers drift across her bra and knowingly search for the bump of a nipple—a blind man learning to read again.

"She shoved me away and slapped my face. We didn't speak as I drove her home and I was certain the relationship was over, but the next day she called and invited me to dinner with her parents. This was a milestone; never before had I been asked to meet them. Dinner consisted of meatloaf. I had been warned long ago to get a good look at a woman's mother as a glimpse into her probable future. I shuddered and prayed not. Her mother was ghoulish—a squatty toad of a woman with a complexion cultivated before the advent of

Pro-Activ. Her father was a meek man who stared into the distance and artificially smiled at random moments.

"At the end of the night the toad took me aside and asked, 'Do you plan on marrying my daughter?'

"'Yes,' I answered.

"'Good,' the toad whispered. 'Make it soon.'

"That night I took her home and while we were kissing on the couch she unfastened her bra and let my hands explore. It should have been an erotic moment, but I couldn't help imagining warts as I brushed against her erect nipples. She bit my lower lip so hard that I cried out and then she whispered into my ear, 'I love you.'

"'Me too,' I mumbled, wondering what I got myself into.

"Two weeks later she took me to Zale's and showed me the engagement ring she wanted. She acted surprised and cried when I dropped to a knee and presented it to her a week later.

"In two months we were married and while she slipped into a pink negligee in the bathroom, I was apprehensive.

"I hadn't dared to venture any lower than her belly button and suddenly I wondered what awaited me between her legs. She was a virgin, of that I was certain, so I assumed she was unaltered by STDs, but I also had visions of some hidden horror. She flipped off the light and moved in the shadows while I had visions of her mother's teeth.

"She slid into the bed next to me and her hands found me beneath the covers. She was far too rough, but she managed to coax me to life. I worked up the courage to investigate my fears and thankfully there were no teeth. I pushed into her softly and then with force. She cried out then took my finger into her mouth and bit into it. I ignored the pain until she was done and then went into the bathroom and wrapped a bandage around my ring finger.

"She had bitten it down to the bone.

"The next night while we were making love for the second time, she tried to pull my injured finger into her mouth and

I pulled it away. She leapt out of bed and wrapped herself with a sheet and ran into the bathroom and locked the door and wept loudly. No amount of coaxing could convince her to come out until the next morning.

"She refused all subsequent romantic advances. I would lie in bed next to her and listen to her soft breathing and stare at the gentle heaving of her chest beneath the covers. Sometimes, I dared a glimpse beneath the sheets; she was lovely. My longing grew until a month later I finally gave in and put my fingers to her lips. She smiled and gently sucked it while I pulled off her panties and rammed into her. At the moment of climax she bit my finger clean off and my golden band slid from the nub and tinkered onto the floor.

"The next day I told co-workers that I had an unfortunate accident with a power saw. I began to wear turtlenecks and often walked with a limp. I had an excuse for every bruise and my friends and family merely nodded at me knowingly.

"She loved me. She reminded me of that during the most painful moments. On our first anniversary she bit off the littlest toe on my left foot and she brought up oral sex. Dr. Phil said that it was a healthy part of a committed relationship. I wondered. I began to drink heavily and developed a litany of excuses to avoid intimacy: work has been hard, I'm tired, I've got headaches, I don't feel sexy. I'm weak from blood loss. None of my reasons satisfied her.

"One day I came home and a trail of rose petals led from the front door all the way to the bedroom. Dozens of candles lit up the room and she was wearing a wife beater T-shirt and no panties. I felt my guts tighten and tears came to my eyes. She was holding a rubber band. She smiled and said, 'We loop it around the left one and once the blood flow is cut off you won't feel a thing.'

"'But . . . but . . . but . . . we want children,' I stammered.

"It was a long night.

"Over the years we became distant. She was the same person I married but I had less and less to give to the relationship. One day she asked for a divorce. I was at a loss. I had come to rely upon her for income because I was wheelchair bound. I had no hands to feed myself and no legs beyond my boney knees. I was fully castrated long before and was in need of testosterone shots to put any semblance of base back into my voice. Only she could understand the crude words I barely managed to verbalize with no tongue. I begged her to stay, but she already made up her mind. Without her I had nothing left. As a final gesture of good will she agreed to put me in this bathtub and turn on the water. I watched her leave as the tub slowly filled around me. I closed my eyes and recalled every sexual position in the Kama Sutra.

"By the time I got to Churning Curds I was fully submerged."

The trickling stopped.

Clint stared at the shower curtain for several minutes and then stood and pulled it back.

The bathtub was empty.

Clint closed the door to the third room and realized he was in a dark place. Whoever had been speaking to him behind the shower curtain was not a part of the living world. Call it a ghost or a trapped memory or a damned soul. There wasn't enough money in the world for him to stay in the building a moment longer. Clint held his fear in check and calmly walked down the corridor and returned to the apartment manager's office. He stared at the stenciled letters: Apart Anger. He rapped on the door several times and waited.

Earl did not open it.

He walked over to the entrance and twisted the knob. It was locked. Clint felt a fight or flight instinct coursing through him. He considered throwing his body against the door until it either flew off its hinges or he was reduced to a bloody stain like the moth in Apartment 2.

He considered sitting down on the marble floor and crying for his mother—except he was no longer a child and his mother had been dead for decades. His mind raced and the best sense he could make of the situation was that Earl must have given each of the tenants a key to the front door so that it could be locked at night; maybe it was some sort of HUD regulation to keep out stragglers since there wasn't a security gate.

Yes, Clint thought, *except it's locked from the outside. We are the stragglers.*

As he saw it, he had two options: go upstairs and get Earl to let him out or walk over to Apartment 4 and hope the tenant was more substantial than the ghost behind the shower curtain or the bloody moth and less insane than the woman in Apartment 1. No doubt the place was as malign as they come, but had he been in any real danger?

He decided to go to the fourth apartment and get the tenant to let him out and, afterward, he'd have a hell of a war story for the other exterminators. No way they'd believe any of it, and Jenn less than anybody.

"Okay."

No, he wouldn't bother telling her anything at all.

THREE

GLUTTONY

The only antidote to mental suffering is physical pain.

~Karl Marx

Chapter Nine
Body Dysmorphia

CLINT WALKED AWAY from Apartment 4 and struggled to silence the echoes of hysterical laughter and tried to forget the blood and the gore and the steady stream of angry insects. Clint stepped up to the pink stairway and saw a boy sitting on the bottom step with his head held low and a Houston Astros hat dipped down over his forehead. The boy glanced up and Clint could see he had been badly beaten. His eyes were swollen and rimmed with various shades of purple and green. His left check was similarly bruised and his lower lip was bleeding. He wore a white Hanes T-shirt and blue jeans that covered most of his body, but his forearms revealed several bruises that trailed out of sight. The boy couldn't have been more than thirteen or fourteen— only a thin shadow of a mustache hinting at approaching manhood.

The boy had been crying—a single tear betrayed him as it trickled down his left cheek.

Clint knelt down next to him, careful not to hover above him lest it intimidate him, and softly asked, "Are you all right?"

The boy smiled weakly and said, "Sure, I'm okay."

Okay. Had there ever been a time in Clint's life when the word didn't seem so loaded with hidden meaning? Had the word ever been genuine or was it always the verbal equivalent of a cyanide pill waiting to be bitten down upon when all other options had been exhausted.

"I think I've been inadvertently trapped in here," Clint said. He rattled the ring of keys and added, "I don't have a key to the front door."

"I know how you feel."

Clint nodded and asked, "Did you get into a fight?"

"No."

The boy didn't look like he could hold his own against a stiff breeze. His arms were thin and the T-shirt hung on him loosely. Clint could empathize—he hadn't started to put on any muscle until he was almost seventeen. He had to wolf down countless protein shakes and handfuls of amino acids, and lift weights like a mad man to finally resemble his idea of real masculinity. Clint grew up feeling puny, insignificant and, worst of all, afraid.

Clint reflexively reached out to pat the boy on the shoulder and the boy flinched. Clint pulled back and mumbled, "Sorry."

The boy forced an apologetic smile; it was heartbreaking.

"Do you have a key to the front door?" Clint asked.

"No."

"Hmm," Clint considered. "I guess I need to go upstairs and get the apartment manager. Or, do you think your parents have one?"

The boy shook his head and said, "He wouldn't give it to me. Besides, I'm giving him some space right now. He's been drinking."

Clint stood and stared down at the boy and asked, "Did your father do that to you?"

"It isn't his fault," the boy explained. "I told you, he's drunk."

Clint felt a heat in his cheeks and realized he was clinching his fists as he stood above the boy. He took a step back and stretched his fingers. "You know that's bullshit, right? That's not an excuse."

The boy looked up at him and shrugged.

Clint thought about Jenn; she would be back at their house propped up in the bed with her feet elevated atop two pillows. Her hand resting on her belly, feeling their son roll around inside her. How could anyone hurt something that was a part of them?

The boy struggled to his feet and leaned against a wall for support and said, "It's better if you don't try to get out."

"What do you mean?"

"It's better to go with the flow," the boy explained. "The more you resist, the harder it's going to push back."

"I don't understand."

"You will," the boy said as he stepped aside and gestured up at the winding staircase.

"What apartment do you live in?" Clint asked. "I'll call the cops or CPS. Hell, I'll talk to your father myself."

"What would that change?" the boy asked.

It will though, Clint thought. *I'll put my boot down on that fucker's throat and tell him if he ever touches the boy again that I'll come back.*

But would he come back to this place, filled with insanity and ghosts and memories he pushed back until they seemed more like stories he heard someone else tell? Would he really come back?

One thing was certain: he wasn't going to stay here any longer than he had to. He'd go up and get a key from the manager and find out what apartment the boy lived in as well.

That much he would do.

He stepped up to the boy and reached out and gently touched the side of his face that wasn't bruised. This time the boy didn't flinch. He stared into the boy's soft eyes and somewhere in there he could see his own reflection.

"It's going to be okay."

Clint reached the top of the pink stairs and the surface shifted back into dark obsidian. Clint stared closely at the dark surface and realized that within were several glittery stones and tiny, swirling fossils of snail shells. He dropped to his knees and studied it closer and could see diatoms of various shapes and sizes like inert snowflakes. He wondered if the surface held the remnants of life that existed millions of years before—forever suspended in the heated volcanic glass. Suspended like the man below in the bathtub.

He stood and felt an even greater urgency to leave this place. He had a wife and an unborn child waiting for him at home.

Earl told Clint that he lived in Apartment 5, so he walked down the long hallway and stepped in front of the door. Somewhere down the hallway dogs were frantically barking.

A thought occurred to Clint just then. *I need a drink. Need one.* It was a persistent thought during times of stress— an escape mechanism that had served him poorly yet never fully lost its appeal.

His affair with alcohol began when he was fifteen during a sleepover with a friend. They raided his father's liquor cabinet and poured a little bit of alcohol out of several bottles and then carefully replaced the missing amounts with water. It was a ridiculous glass filled with whiskey, gin, vodka, and tequila; when his friend took a gulp he turned pale and ran into the bathroom and vomited. Clint sipped it slowly and it burned going down, but it also lit a fire in his bones and calmed his mind. The more he drank, the quieter the persistent voices in his head became. Sometimes they were silenced altogether. It was like being reborn, absent the burden that time and circumstance slowly heaps upon a person until the weight of it seems unbearable. A baptism with all sins forgiven and a chance to never make them again.

As Clint grew older he realized the sins don't truly go

away, you just quit caring about them when you are submerged deeply enough beneath the cleansing waters.

Clint promised Jenn he'd quit drinking, and he tried. He went to AA meetings and he read books. He set up a work area in the garage and spent his idle time building a train set. He set up a track on a long table and painted each car with a magnifying glass in one hand and a tiny paintbrush in the other. Next, he built a schoolhouse that sat just off the tracks and he painted each window with delicate detail and afterward he added a church and then a courthouse. There were tiny figurines as well: families, policemen, businessmen, firemen, and most importantly the conductor.

He drank Dr. Pepper while he worked and avoided smoking as best as he could because smoking and drinking are soul mates.

He was painting a tunnel when Jenn rushed into the garage. She was crying and before he could ask why she blurted out, "I'm pregnant."

"I'm so happy," he said. And he was, but he had gone for a drive that night and pulled into a convenience store and bought a six-pack of Budweiser tallboys. After the fourth can he tossed his six month sobriety chip out the window and laughed. He bought another six-pack before he came home and when he stumbled into bed Jenn lay as still as a corpse and the next morning she left for work without saying goodbye.

As the months passed he realized he was spiraling, and only after she threatened to leave him did he finally agree to quit again. For good, this time. He imagined living without his wife, the only person who had ever stood beside him, and that was enough to set him straight. Clint had abandonment issues and his wife knew it. It was her final chip to play.

Jenn resented having to play it, she told him.

He resented her for playing it.

He dusted off the train set and set up a dark tunnel that the train rushed into and then out of—a perpetual loop while the buildings and tiny people watched in silent judgment.

They Don't Check Out

I need a drink.

Clint rapped insistently on the apartment manager's door. Silence.

Where was that fat asshole? Clint banged on the door for a good ten seconds and waited. No answer and no sounds from within.

Clint pulled out his key ring and opened the door.

The kitchen was orderly and clean and the cupboards were stacked with the foundation of a fairly decent health food store: quinoa, Gold Standard Whey powder, spirulina, Thermonex energy capsules, muesli, gluten free bread, and Nutella. The refrigerator was stacked with Humus and Tofurkey and a plethora of vegan meat substitutes.

Clint was suddenly certain that Earl Guin had lied about the apartment he lived in; he stepped into the living room and he was certain of it.

Several framed photographs lined the walls and the common man in all of them could not have been more different than the apartment manager; he was a tall muscular man with a chiseled jaw and disarmingly blue eyes. The kind of man women spoke about in whispers when their husbands weren't around. In one photograph his golden hair hung at his shoulders and he posed next to a fine looking couple that Clint assumed was his parents. His father had that same strong, dimpled jaw and broad shoulders; however, his hair was silver and time had marked his face with graceful valleys. The woman had full lips and flowing blonde hair and the same striking blue eyes as her son. They were all three impossibly perfect, as if God had created them and then Photoshopped out any of the numerous human frailties. It was a stock graduation photo and the man stood with a rolled up diploma in one hand and his other arm was wrapped around his father's waist.

In another photograph he stood on a beach next to several other tanned boys and girls. A koozie in his left hand hid what had to be a beer and his other arm was wrapped around a brunette with full breasts and naughty intentions judging from the size of her bikini. There were two other boys posed behind him, but they shrank into the background; his ripped abdomen and massive upper body brought the world into focus. Clint figured it was Spring Break and he envied the drinking and fucking and promise held within that static shot. Photographs are like frozen memories, trapped in time forever, and that was a fine one.

In another photograph his long thick hair had been buzzed down and he was dressed in a camouflaged uniform with an American flag patch sewn into the shoulders. His posture was erect and his smile had faded. His stare was intense and threatening. Spring Break was over.

Clint focused on another photograph; the man had aged considerably. He wore a black military uniform with red pinstripes and large golden buttons that ran down from his chin. His chest was adorned with medals and several multicolored patches had been sewn into his jacket. One of his pants legs ended at the knee.

Clint wondered if the handsome man in the photograph could possibly be . . . No, that was impossible. Earl was at least a foot shorter than the man in the photograph and his face was disfigured. The missing leg must be some sort of strange coincidence.

Clint sprayed the living room, and then moved into a bedroom. There was a bed that had been made to suit military inspection with white sheets and a red quilt perfectly tucked and pillows neatly placed. The only other item in the bedroom was a huge standing full-body mirror that looked like it had come from the 1800s. In front of the mirror sat a digital scale. The barren room was painted black.

Clint realized a soft sound was coming from the closet.

Whimpering and then the barely audible whisper, "Bug Man."

Clint thought of the boy with the bruise on his face as he slowly opened the door.

A man was crouched in the back of the closet. He seemed to have just stepped out of the last photograph—he wore the black military uniform adorned with his accomplishments. Tears streamed down his face and he was inconsolable.

"Are you okay?" Clint asked.

The man ignored him and leaned against the wall and struggled up to his feet.

Feet, Clint thought. *Unlike the last photograph, he still had two legs.* The man reached up to a shelf situated above neatly pressed suits and pants that hung on a metal bar. The man reached into a metal box and withdrew a gun.

Clint quickly stepped back. It was a 1911 pistol.

"What are you doing?" Clint asked, but the man stepped past him as if he were non-existent.

Tears streamed from the man's eyes and there was something strange about the way he walked, as if one of his legs had fallen asleep.

The man stepped in front of the mirror and stared into its endless depths. His sorrow intensified. He turned away and placed his gun on the edge of the bed and slowly unbuttoned his jacket.

Clint remained perfectly still, fully aware that the man was a trained killer held in the throes of some great anguish. The man folded his jacket and placed it on the bed next to the gun. He took off a white T-shirt and placed it next to the jacket. His torso was still muscular and impressive though his belly was no longer flat and there was a hint of love handles at his hips. He unbuckled his belt and sat down next to the gun. He took off his shoes and socks.

Two feet.

Slowly the man pulled down his pants—one of his legs was a metallic pole with an amazingly life-like foot attached to the end. The man folded his pants and laid them next to the other clothes and then he took off his prosthetic leg and tossed it on the floor. It made a heavy thud. He pulled down his underwear and folded them next to the pants.

The man rose to one leg and picked up the gun. He hopped over to the mirror, and then took a final tentative leap onto the scale. "Please," the man softly muttered.

He stared down at the scale and seeing the digital number, he sobbed.

He opened his mouth and placed the barrel of the 1911 past his lips.

"Stop," Clint shouted.

He squeezed the trigger and the gunshot echoed.

He collapsed in front of the mirror and twisted as if he was hooked up to electrodes receiving electroshock therapy.

Then he was still.

Clint walked over and knelt down and took the 1911 out of his hand. He unclasped his satchel and tucked the 1911 in it beside a bait-gun.

Clint glanced at the mirror and gasped.

Within the depths he could see Earl Guin slowly hopping toward him.

Clint ran out of the living room and he did not slow down to study the framed photographs, but from the corner of his eyes he could see that the handsome man had been replaced by a familiar grotesque figure. Clint understood then about the scar he had mistaken as the remnants of a severe hair lip.

The kitchen counter was covered with bags of Lay's potato chips and cases of Pepsi and Mountain Dew. Clint didn't slow down to see what sort of junk food now filled the pantry or refrigerator and he didn't stop running until he had stumbled into the hallway and slammed the kitchen door behind him. He was certain Earl Guin had hopped out of the mirror, leapt over the corpse, and was even now hopping toward him.

Chapter Ten
Cultural Solution

THE BOY HAD warned Clint that it was better to go with the flow; and if doing so was to remain trapped then he was compliant, because yet again he had failed to obtain a key to the front door. Clint stepped up to Apartment 6 and grasped a doorknocker shaped like a hand. He lifted the metal hand and slammed it against the door. There was movement inside and a second later the door opened a crack—it was chained from the inside. An elderly black man with nervous eyes asked, "What do you want?"

"Pest control," Clint said.

"I thought I heard a gunshot or a goddamned bottle rocket being fired off in the hallway. Is there anyone else out there?"

"No. Mr. Guin sent me."

"The fat man?"

"Yes, sir."

"Sir?" he asked. His voice softened and he added, "Come on in." He unfastened the chain.

Clint stepped into a narrow kitchen and the man quickly refastened the chain. The man had an air of sophistication with sharp eyes, and a well-trimmed silver mustache that framed thick lips. He wore a black suit with a matching tie that held up a double chin and loose jowls. His hair was cut short and heavily salted with age and experience. Clint pegged him as a high priced attorney or maybe a televangelist.

He extended a hand and said, "Kermit James, pleased to make your acquaintance."

"Clint Stern." His hand was soft, and his fingernails had been manicured.

"I don't have any bugs; I keep a clean house."

Clint glanced around the kitchen and noted that the counters shone. He nodded in agreement and said, "Maybe I should spray anyway. You might catch some strays from your neighbors."

"Neighbors? I suppose so. I'm embarrassed to say I've never met them. I must seem anti-social."

"Not at all. Do I smell cigar?"

Kermit smiled and said, "You do. Just one of my numerous vices. I apologize if the smell bothers you. After my wife left me I quit worrying about other people's needs. My wife would tell you I've always been a narcissist. Maybe. I've never been reliable at self-diagnosis."

"Been there," Clint said and he opened a cabinet and sprayed behind a box of oatmeal. "You're in good company with me. Not only do I not mind the smell of cigar, I used to smoke them."

"Used to?"

"Yeah," Clint said. He smiled and added, "My wife hasn't left me yet."

"Yet," Kermit said and he laughed. "Good for you. Give her time."

"Don't let me interrupt you," Clint said and he stepped into the living room; it was furnished as finely as a study in an upscale law office. An oak table sat in front of a bookcase and on it was an ashtray that held a fat cigar which emitted a slow trickle of glorious smoke. Clint stared at a bottle of Parker's Heritage Bourbon that sat next to the ashtray. There was a shotglass by the bottle.

"You want to piss off your wife?"

"What?" The question shocked Clint and he turned and Kermit was standing next to him, a broad smile on his distinguished face.

"Have a cigar with me. I don't meet many aficionados anymore and would love to chat you up. I've been trying to work through a box of Don Arturo's and you'd be doing me a favor."

"I shouldn't," Clint said.

"Shouldn't you? Don't worry, I won't tell the fat man."

"What the hell," Clint said. "I appreciate it."

Kermit went to the bookshelf and opened an ornate humidor and pulled out a cigar banded in red and gold. He carefully snipped the tip with a metal cutter and handed it to Clint, along with a gold torch lighter.

Clint put the cigar to his lips and slowly twisted it as he held it in front of him. It tasted like heaven and as he exhaled he watched the smoke slowly billow toward the ceiling.

"It's like sex, right?"

"Kind of," Clint admitted. "Maybe more like masturbation."

Kermit laughed. "Good one. Good for you. I know just what you mean too. An irresistible, God-given urge, followed by shame and regret." Kermit poured a shot of bourbon, swallowed it in one gulp, and quickly lifted his cigar and took an enormous puff that clouded his face. He sat down and pointed at a chair and said, "Sit down, friend, and let's talk about regrettable sins."

Clint sat and his gaze settled on the bottle of 96 proof bourbon.

"How rude of me," Kermit said and he quickly poured a shot. "Smoking a cigar absent a good bourbon is a sin."

He poured the shot glass and slid it in front of Clint.

Clint tried to formulate a polite way to decline the offer and independent of his own thoughts his hand reached down and took the shot glass and he drank it.

It burned him like a first kiss, warmed his chest, and reminded him that he was alive.

I'm alive.

"I've got to warn you," Clint said. "Whiskey tends to make me mean spirited."

"No worries," Kermit said. "This is the good stuff."

"You want to talk about shame and regret?" Clint asked. "Regrettable sins? Here's one for you. It might seem slight, but it impacted me.

"I was nineteen years old and I had gone to a fraternity kegger. I was driving home totally blitzed. I was scared shitless of getting a DWI because you've never seen cops until you've lived in a college town. They had a hard-on for giving out DWIs and it seemed like every other car on the highway was either local police, UPD, or highway patrol. I was trying my damnedest not to weave and I remember staring at the speedometer and trying to keep it at fifty-five on the dot—speed and they'll pull you over. Go too slow and they'll pull you over even quicker.

"I glanced at the road just as I hit a small animal. At first, I was sure it was a squirrel or maybe a raccoon or an armadillo. I quickly realized it was bigger than that.

"There were typically a lot of deer out at night and it wasn't too uncommon to find a carcass on the side of the road the next day, but it had been smaller than that. I made a U-turn and went back and saw it in a grassy ditch off the side of the road.

"It was a border collie. You know Lassie?"

"Sure I do. The dog that always came home."

"Yeah, it was that kind of dog. Beautiful long hair and soft eyes. A loyal fucking dog. I had one when I was a kid and loved it—it slept on the foot of my bed every night and somehow I felt safer with it next to me. Anyway, this one was fucked; I could see that right off. It was trying to drag itself further away from the road, but its back legs wouldn't work. It looked like my wheels had crushed its entire lower half because it was thinner and . . . " Clint poured a shot of whiskey and swallowed it. "It had intestines coming out of its ass. I try to forget that detail, but I can't. It saw my headlights and stared at me and I'm sure it couldn't see me, but it seemed like it could. I was wasted and in that moment I figured it was looking into my eyes and begging me to help it."

"What did you do?"

"What could I do? It was going to die; no way a vet could have saved it. Besides, if I stuck around a cop would have driven by and I would have been fucked. I drove away and left it to die."

"That's not so bad," Kermit said. "Hell, it was an accident. Nothing you could do."

"I told myself that," Clint agreed, "but it's a lie. I wondered all night if it was out there suffering all alone. Alone. Even now that dog is out there in that ditch waiting for me to do the right thing."

"You said yourself it was too far gone for a vet. It was bound to die."

"True," Clint agreed. "And that part doesn't bother me. Death is natural and I accept that. If it had died then—or four years later—it was headed toward the same fate. My border collie, his name was Jordan. He had been put to sleep three years before that and I held him when the vet gave him the shot. I cried, but it was a kind and respectful end. It was merciful.

"Death I can understand but not suffering. I had a tire iron in the back of my truck. I could have put him down quick with one, maybe two licks. I could have been merciful. Should have."

"You are wrong about that," Kermit said. "Suffering is just as natural as death. In fact, they are twins on opposite ends of a spectrum."

"No," Clint argued. "The opposite of death is life."

"That's my point. Life is suffering. Same thing."

Clint considered and then slowly nodded. "I can't disagree with that, but why is that dog still dying on the side of the road every time I am reminded of it?"

The man laughed without humor and said, "So that you'll suffer. That dog has been dead for years—the only place that it's still alive is in your head. Maybe that's the price you pay for your mistake. Maybe that's your way of keeping it alive.

"Bug Man, you want to know what I did for a living?"

Clint poured another shot and swished it like mouthwash before he swallowed it. "Sure. I figured you for a lawyer."

"Close. I was a doctor. My practice was located not too far from here in Jasper. I ran a place called Delta Clinic that specialized in providing services for poor women—mostly blacks and illegal immigrants. Now, I don't know if you are familiar with clinics that specialize in services for poor minorities, but the funding is pretty piss poor. Now, the things that Medicaid wouldn't provide for, I had to do them on the cheap."

"Wait a second," Clint said. "Are you telling me you are a doctor and living in this hellhole?" Clint quickly added, "No offense. I mean, your apartment is lavish. I'm speaking specifically about this complex."

"No offense taken," Kermit said. "This place is horrible and back in the day I lived a good life. A two-story house, a BMW hummer, and a fine wife twenty years my junior who shaved her pussy and thought anal sex was foreplay. I lost all of that shortly after my medical license was suspended and I was put on trial."

"For what?"

"Well, that's a longer story. What you have to understand is bad things don't usually happen in a flash. They happen in degrees. Increments so subtle that you aren't even aware that your life is sloping down instead of up. I was a good doctor and I ran that clinic because I came from nothing and I wanted to give back. My upbringing was a goddamned cliché: poor black boy raised by his grandmother. No idea who my father was and my mother was in and out of my life when she wasn't high. I decided not to be another cliché, so I worked my ass off to rise out of poverty. I became fucking Bill Cosby—you know Dr. Huxtable?"

"Yeah, I remember that."

"What you didn't learn on the Cosby show is a lot of

people don't want to go to a black doctor—not a lot of white people, anyway."

"And black people in the South don't tend to be that well off financially," Clint added.

"Right. I also had an agenda. I'll admit that freely. I had at least six siblings from six different fathers that I couldn't identify in a police lineup. Poverty and procreation—a wicked combo. I decided to do my part to end the cycle as well. We gave out free condoms and gave our best speeches on safe sex, but my real specialty was abortions. I'm known around these parts by the moniker "Abortion Doctor," and if I have a legacy that is it. I performed hundreds of them—like a fucking assembly line those poor scared young women came into my office and they left with one less burden to consider."

"I respect that," Clint said. "I always thought it was way too easy to have a child. You have to pass a test to drive, but any asshole can have a kid."

"Right. And even easier for a man to put his seed in some random woman and disappear forever. You talk about your shame at leaving that dog out there to suffer for another hour or so, but where is the shame of thousands of men that leave their children out there for a lifetime? I fixed that.

"I was proud of it too. Each abortion gave me a sense of satisfaction, like I was part of a cultural solution. The problem is those increments I told you about. I started off doing first trimester abortions only—nothing past fourteen weeks. It was ethical and justifiable, but you wouldn't believe how many women I was shoving out the door. Were they left with no alternative but to get a backroom abortion by some fool with a coat hanger, or worse, were they having those unwanted babies? Repeating the familiar destructive cycle?

"I couldn't live with that. Toward the end I was operating on women in their third trimester. Babies with fingers and toes. The first time I heard one of them cry, I nearly shit myself. Eventually it got easier—a snip of surgical scissors on their spines and lights out. I felt like I was doing God's work.

I really did. I became addicted to the whole process. I got a thrill from each underprivileged child I kept out of this world. It got to the point where I'd abort a child under any circumstance. Due date soon? Whatever. It gave me a sense of control over my own past and provided the illusion that I was an important cog in an orderly universe, not just an inconsequential soul trapped amidst random chaos. I was right, and I was also wrong. There is order, but I was never in control of it. I had become a glutton to my basest desire and what I fooled myself into thinking was selfless service was actually just a sick way of feeding my own fragile ego. I was a murderer. I see that now so clearly. Back then I still felt justified.

"It wasn't until the first woman bled out that I came under any real scrutiny. And then . . . well, you can see the end right in front of you. My hand is so shaky that I couldn't hold a scalpel if I had to. I gave away the last of my equipment to a woman who lives beneath us. Good riddance."

"Increments," Clint said softly.

"Yeah," Kermit agreed. "That's how it works. Life isn't about learning or doing good. It's just a steady decaying of everything in you that's worthwhile until the only thing left is . . . suffering."

Clint rose to his feet unsteadily and said, "I've got to go."

"You don't have to," Kermit insisted. "You and I are the same." He poured two more shots of whiskey and said, "I can't forget, but this helps a bit to dull the guilt."

Clint shook his head and said, "I'm sorry, but we aren't the same.

Kermit nodded his head slowly and said, "You wouldn't be here if we weren't. You see, that's part of the order. I can see it now and given enough time, so will you. The only thing worse than suffering is doing it alone."

"No," Clint insisted. "I'm not like you at all. We both drink too much. Fine, I'll own that, but the rest of it . . . "

They Don't Check Out

Clint walked to the front door and turned and glanced back at Kermit. He was staring down at his hands. Clint left the apartment and only after he closed the door behind him was he reminded that he forgot to ask for a key to the exit.

Somewhere down the hall a dog barked frantically.

Chapter Eleven
Polaroids

CLINT STOOD IN the hallway and listened as a dog barked with the consistency of a heartbeat. His head was in the soothing embrace of drunkenness and his body felt light and strong. Clint walked down the hallway, back to the stairs he had ascended, and he realized they were gone. There was simply a blank wall and the cold floor beneath him. The only staircase led upward and was as inviting as an electric chair.

The dog continued to bark.

Clint understood this place now—why it held so many tormented souls living and dead. They were paying a price. Penance is the term that came to mind. He wasn't a religious man, but you don't grow up in East Texas without learning some things via osmosis. They were here to repent for their sins.

But why was he here?

Clint sat down at the foot of the stairs and reviewed his sins. Adultery? He cheated on Jenn and he owned it, but that was before they married and never again. Was that even considered a sin? In fact, he was fairly certain that absent marriage it wasn't even considered wrong in the eyes of God—and wasn't He the judge, jury, and executioner?

No, what he had done was cheat on a girlfriend and nothing more. It had been wrong, but the only person he owed an apology to was Jenn, and no one else. And hadn't he paid the price for it? He continued to pay for it every day through sullen glances and tense moments of unprovoked silence.

Somewhere down the hall a dog continued to bark and Clint considered the dog he had left on the side of the highway. Try as he might, Clint couldn't tag that action to any sort of sin he knew about. Hell, if letting an animal suffer was a sin then everyone he knew was damned. In Nacogdoches alone, there were at least a dozen chicken houses filled to capacity with thousands of yard birds pumped up on steroids to the point where they were so oversized that they could no longer walk. Laying in their own feces and waiting for harvest like fleshy ears of corn. Packed into trucks and rushed to the Pilgrim's Pride packaging plant so they could be ripped apart and served as chicken strips and nuggets and pressed patties to the gluttonous masses.

Cows and pigs got it even worse. Clint had heard once that pigs were far smarter than dogs and almost certainly smarter than a lot of people Clint dealt with on a daily basis. If the Bible logic that Clint had grown up on held true then God put animals on the earth for people to use as they saw fit. Given that, he hadn't sinned. Besides, hadn't he already punished himself enough already?

Still the dog incessantly barked.

Why was he here? He could understand why the others were trapped here; that made perfect sense. The man in the bathtub was paying the price for committing himself fully to a relationship and losing his humanity in the process.

Clint could certainly empathize. Sometimes he could see himself through Jenn's eyes and doing so he felt like less of a man.

The woman trapped down there with her aborted children—Clint could understand that as well. What could be more unnatural than a mother who hurts her child? Kermit was the other side of that exact same coin.

The crazy woman filled with bugs? She was just another

victim who embraced her pain until it consumed her. Come to think of it, maybe she and the man in the bathtub were intertwined as well.

Earl was an even more obvious candidate for damnation. Clint had watched that Brad Pitt movie, *Seven*, at least a dozen times and he recognized pride as one of the deadly sins. Add in suicide, and there was little doubt he was right where he belonged.

But why was Clint here? He hadn't done anything worthy of being brought here and besides, he was alive. Wasn't this the sort of punishment reserved for the dead? Maybe this whole thing was some sort of cosmic misunderstanding. A divine fuckup of the highest magnitude.

Wait a second. This wasn't even supposed to be his gig in the first place.

Hollis.

This had to be meant for him. In an attempt to help out a friend Clint had inadvertently stepped into his madness. No good deed goes unpunished. No shit. If that saying wasn't biblical, then it should have been.

Clint smiled with the sudden realization that he was going to be okay. He'd do his damnedest to play by whatever sick rules governed the reality he stumbled into and then he'd get out and go home. If there was a lesson to be taken from this, then he'd learn it. Clint had never believed in hell, but his mind had been changed in that regard.

Nothing but clean living from now on.

Clint smiled. He would put down his head and regard whatever horrors he faced like a child moving through a haunted house on Halloween, suspending disbelief, but always cognizant that the monsters weren't real. He would hold onto his reality by spraying each apartment until he fulfilled his obligation and then he'd leave.

Clint pulled out his pack of Marlboros, lit a cigarette, and walked to Apartment 7.

The incessant barking was coming from within.

Clint took a final drag from his cigarette and casually tossed it on the floor. He hesitated before he rapped on the door, wondering why the tenant had been trapped in there. One thing was certain—they all shared a sort of group delusion. Clint would compliantly play along in his role as pest control technician.

Clint gently rapped on the door.

The barking sounded like it was coming from inches away—perhaps the dog was pressed against the door, trying to chew its way out. A moment later the door opened a crack and a man asked, "How can I help you?" His voice was almost drowned out by the frantic barking.

"I'm here to spray."

"I'll need to put my dogs in the kennel," the man shouted. "They aren't fond of strangers. Give me a minute."

"Sure."

There was a bit of rustling around inside and the man screamed, "Move it, you fucker," and a dog yelped. A moment later the door opened and the man said, "Okay, come on in."

Barking filled the apartment.

Clint quickly treated the kitchen and moved into the living room. The man was seated at a computer desk in front of a monitor and across the room sat an enormous kennel that held three Rottweilers who were so similar that they could have been clones. Certainly they had come from the same litter. For a moment, due to their close proximity within the kennel, Clint imagined it was one dog with three heads. The dogs barked in perfect unison, further enhancing the illusion they shared a single consciousness.

The man quickly turned off the monitor and asked, "Are these chemicals safe around the dogs?"

"Yes."

The man was middle-aged with skin as pale and pleasant as a nest of writhing maggots. He wore thick glasses and was dressed in tan slacks and a striped polo shirt.

Clint sprayed the baseboards but gave the kenneled

Rottweilers a wide berth. Their barking had not slowed a bit. Their mouths frothed with hatred as they watched Clint. Several stuffed animals were arranged on a shelf next to a model of the Millennium Falcon and dozens of children's books. Clint moved to the back of the apartment and, finding the bedroom door closed, he shouted, "Is there anyone in there?"

"No, Bug Man," the man shouted from the living room.

Clint stepped inside and closed the door behind him. Still, he could hear the dull bass of the dogs' complaints. Clint was drawn toward the closet, hopeful that no one was hidden within. Slowly he opened the door. Empty.

The closet was filled with clothing that would have met Mr. Rogers's approval. Clint quickly sprayed the baseboards and as he reached out to close the closet a shoebox fell off the top shelf and spilled its contents at his feet.

Polaroids. Dozens. Boys and girls, none older than ten or eleven, and no more than two children captured within each picture. Most of the children were naked. Their eyes were red. Fear. Shame. Some of the pictures had been taken in the living room, only a few feet away.

Clint lifted a photograph and turned it over. Samantha.

There was a name written on the back of each picture, printed in black ballpoint ink by the same steady hand. Dennis. Christy. Toby. Jamal. These children were elsewhere now, hopefully somewhere safe, far away from the man who waited in the living room. But the moments represented in each Polaroid would live with them until they died and maybe even beyond. It happened.

Clint gathered the moments, stacked them, and placed them inside the box. He returned the box to the shelf, closed the closet door, and left the sad, naked children behind.

The dogs were still barking.

Clint opened the door to the living room and the little man quickly turned off the computer monitor and swiveled around in his chair. He smiled and asked, "All done?"

"Yeah," Clint mumbled. "What are you doing on the computer?"

The little man's eyes shifted nervously and he said, "Lesson planning. I'm a preschool teacher. I was updating my hug chart."

Clint removed the tank from his back, one strap at a time, and sat it down at his feet.

The little man squirmed in his chair and glanced across the room at the kennel. "Don't bother," Clint said. "Your dogs are fine in there."

"I don't know what you think you know," the little man said. "What did you find? The pictures?"

"Yeah."

"Did you consider for a moment that they are far more innocent than you might be . . . aware of?" The little man shrunk lower into his chair until it seemed that he might flow into the fabric and disappear altogether. "Those pictures are clinical in nature, acquired from the school nurse who checks anyone suspected of being abused at home. I am merely keeping them in case anything ever—"

"Bullshit," Clint said. "Some of those pictures were taken in this apartment. What were you doing bringing children here?"

The little man shrugged, feigning bravado and said, "So, you think you know everything, huh?"

"Yeah, I do."

"And I'm sure you are standing there in judgment, like most of the others."

"Most?" Clint asked and he suddenly realized he had subconsciously unzipped his satchel and his hand was tucked inside. His palm had settled upon the butt of the 1911.

"Certainly," the little man said. "Not everyone is so closed-minded. It's not as one-sided as you'd like to think either. Society tells them that it's not good to have a relationship with older people and to suppress their desires."

Clint spat and said, "Children."

The little man fidgeted in the chair, searching for words. "You can't be too young for sex. Everything you like—no matter what age you are—you don't stop liking as you get older. It's only indoctrination that makes people not like things or get embarrassed by them. Like if a very young child is masturbated by a family—"

Clint pulled the gun out of the satchel and pointed it at the little man and screamed, "I know why you are here." Clint paused as if deep in thought and then mumbled, "And now I think I know why I'm here. My wife is . . . I know why I'm here."

The dogs sounded furious now and they threw their bodies against the metal bars of the kennel.

The little man raised his arms and said, "It's no different than a child sitting on a grandpa's lap or being hugged. It's only people that make it taboo."

Clint took a step forward and aimed the gun at the little man's forehead. He imagined a bullet passing just above his right eye and washing the monitor with his brains.

"I'm not the worst," the little man screamed. "Not even close. It's society that gives them mental problems because they convince them it's wrong."

Retribution, Clint thought. *That's why I'm here.* God's work. How foolish to think it could have been a mistake. God brought him here for a purpose. He was chosen. A man who had been . . . A man with a pregnant wife at home. A son waiting to be born into a world with people like this in it. God had called in an exterminator to take out an infestation.

"I'm going to kill you," Clint said.

"No," the man shouted. "It's against the rules. Hell, it's the only rule. It won't let you."

Clint took a step forward and struck the man with the gun's barrel. His nose caved inward and opened like a bloody mouth. The little man fell to his knees and screamed. Clint struck him again with the barrel of the gun and his cheek cracked like handmade pottery.

The man went facedown and then slowly crawled on his belly toward the kennel, mumbling, "The others will come."

"No," Clint said. "I'm coming for them."

The pedophile glanced back and grinned. His face resembled a decaying jack-o-lantern. Clint took a step forward and stomped the back of the little man's head and felt the skull shift beneath his boot. Teeth flew and skittered on the floor.

The little man gurgled as he desperately tried to pull himself toward the kennel. Clint stomped the back of his head until the little man was still and then several more times for good measure. Only the broken glasses hinted at humanity amid the gore.

The dogs were silent.

Clint stared at them as they passively waved their stumpy tails. Their ribs poked into tight skin and their muscles were loose. Their fur was thin and patchy. They didn't look like they had eaten in weeks. The bottom of their kennel was lined with small panties and underwear.

Clint aimed the gun at one of the Rottweilers and it licked at the air as its tail continued to wag.

Clint put the bloody 1911 back in the satchel.

Clint reached down and unlocked the kennel and opened it. The dogs cautiously emerged, and two of them went over to the little man and licked at what remained of his face. The third dog stood compliantly next to Clint and stared up at him adoringly.

Clint turned and walked into the kitchen as the tearing sounds began in the living room. The third dog stayed next to him, as close as a shadow.

"Okay," Clint told the dog.

Together they went into the silent hallway and Clint closed the door behind them.

Chapter Twelve
Purge

CLINT LIGHTLY RAPPED on the door of Apartment 8. His hand drifted to the satchel and he thought of the 1911 gently tucked beside the poisonous gels and baits. One thing was certain, he had been sent here to kill.

The door opened and, for a moment, Clint thought he was staring at a child or perhaps a preteen. Then his gaze settled on her face and the echoes of time around her eyes and mouth, and he realized she was merely a very small woman. Less than five feet tall and thin. Her shirt sparkled with gold sequins that spelled out "Sassy" and her pink leggings hung loosely around stork-like legs. She wore green house slippers shaped like cartoon frogs with bubbly eyes that jiggled within their plastic sockets. Her hair was cut like a mushroom cap, a style Dorothy Hamill had once popularized, but now appeared immature and lazy, the stylish equivalent of throwing in the towel on life.

She leaned down and gently stroked the Rottweiler and Clint could see her hair was thinning on top. She looked up curiously and asked, "Is this one of Mr. Anderson's dogs?" Her yellow teeth receded into her mouth as if the enamel was being stripped away layer by layer.

"Mr. Anderson?"

"Yeah, my neighbor down the hall." She scratched the Rottweiler between the ears and said, "You like to bark all night, don't you, boy? But, I don't mind. These walls are as thick as thieves. Only time I hear you is in the hallway." She looked up at Clint and asked, "Did Mr. Anderson give him to you? I always figured three dogs were overkill for apartment living."

"I'm just taking him for a walk," Clint said.

She stood and said, "Good for you. Mr. Anderson could use your help. You should see those dogs dragging him down the hall. Sweet man but in over his head."

"Yeah."

"Come on in. Is it safe for you to spray while I'm eating?"

"Absolutely."

They stepped into the tight kitchen and she said, "I could count the number of roaches I've seen in here on two fingers, but I guess it never hurts to be proactive, right?"

"That's right," Clint agreed.

She shuffled out of the kitchen and Clint sprayed under the refrigerator and placed a few roach baits in cabinets that held pots and pans and Tupperware containers and little else. The pantry closet was stocked with several bags of Cool Ranch Doritos and an entire shelf was filled with Cinnamon Toast Crunch. A metal scale sat on the counter next to a microwave.

Clint stepped into the living room and the woman was seated at a small, round dining table. Three microwave style pizzas and a bag of Nacho Cheese Doritos were arranged in front of her. She glanced up at Clint nervously and he said, "Don't worry. The chemical is absolutely safe."

She smiled and took a single chip out of the Doritos bag and let it rest in her mouth, as if she were waiting for it to melt away.

Clint sprayed the baseboards behind her and then quickly moved through a living room that was furnished with a green vinyl couch, a round Japanese lamp, and a treadmill situated in front of a plasma television that was mounted against the wall.

Clint glanced back at her as he moved into the hallway

and she was still staring at him intently, her mouth partially opened with the chip still carefully nestled within.

"Is it okay if I spray back here as well?"

"Whatever you think, Bug Man."

Clint stepped into the bathroom and sprayed around the edges. The toilet lid was propped open and a wet plunger sat carelessly on the floor next to half a bottle of Listerine. Clint opened the cabinet beneath the sink and felt like he had been transported to aisle five at Walgreens. Dulcolax. Ex-lax. Nature's Remedy. Fleet. Carter's Laxative. Senna.

Clint closed the cabinet and moved into the bedroom. The small room was engulfed by a king-size bed adorned with floral printed throw pillows. Clint sprayed the baseboards and paused in front of the closet. A smell like death was nestled within.

Clint unfastened the satchel and settled his right hand comfortably on the 1911. Clint reached out with his left hand and slowly opened the door.

The closet was filled with large blue Tupperware containers stacked almost four feet high and three feet deep.

Hundreds.

Each of them was labeled.

October 5, 4.4 pounds. October 6, 4.1 pounds. October 7, 4.6 pounds.

Clint lifted one from the back: February 8, 3.8 pounds. The contents within sloshed around. Clint sat the container on the ground and slowly unscrewed the lid. The smell was overwhelming.

The vile liquid within had congealed at the top like the thick skin of a primordial reptile. Clint quickly resealed it and carefully placed the container back between February 7 and 9.

Clint walked back into the living room and said, "All done."

The woman held one of the pizzas in her hands. It was folded over like an enormous taco. The other two pizzas were gone and the Doritos bag was empty. The woman started eating at a bottom corner and, like a buzzard, she took several fierce bites in a row, paused to swallow, and then began the process anew. Tomato sauce squirted out with each bite and dripped down her chin. Within minutes the pizza was gone.

The woman wiped her hands and mouth on her sassy shirt and said, "This is called binging. It's the fun part."

Clint stared at her and slowly nodded.

"The next part," she continued, "is not as fun, but in many ways is far more satisfying. Did you find any pests?"

"None at all."

"I didn't think you would. I keep the place as clean as a hospital. Cleaner even. That's what it used to be. Did you know that?"

Clint nodded.

The woman stepped out of the dining room and disappeared in the kitchen. "I used to be a patient here," she shouted. "Almost twenty years ago. I was just a kid, fifteen years old." She stepped out of the kitchen with a blue Tupperware container gripped in her hands; she sat it on the dining room table.

"Why were you admitted here?" Clint asked, already knowing the truth, but wanting to hear her twisted version of reality.

She sat back down at the dining room table and smiled and said, "I was damn near dead. I weighed fifty pounds when they admitted me. At that point I was restricting myself to three carrot sticks and two saltines a day. Nothing more. At dinner time, I'd stare across the table at my mother and laugh while she begged me to eat. I reminded her that she was the one who called me chubby when I was a little girl. She was the one who sent me to a camp for fat kids. "

"So, were you teaching your mom a lesson?"

"Kind of," she admitted. "Mainly I was taking control. That's one of the things they taught me here. It's all about control. There's not much in this life you have power over, but what goes into your body . . . control. Of course they took that away from me. They inserted a tube directly into my stomach and forced me to eat as much as they wanted. Fattened me up. Made me sit in a circle with the other losers and learn about all of the ways we were broken. They had funny labels for it too. Anorexia Nervosa. That's what I had."

"Had?"

"Yeah, had," she said, smiling. "Throw out the scales. I did that. I haven't weighed myself in years. Quit exercising yourself to death. I did that as well. That treadmill behind you, that's for show. A trophy. This apartment . . . it's a trophy as well. For all I remember, this might even be the same room where I was admitted. My luxurious bed might be in the same room where I was strapped down and force-fed. I like to think it was."

"And now you're cured?"

"Sure, I am," she said. "You ever hear of an anorexic who eats three pizzas at a time? No way. Now I'm doing it my way and would you call me chubby?"

"No."

"Damn right. I shop in the kid's section. This outfit is a size ten and I could fit in an eight, but I like my clothes loose. I learned some tricks here all right. Three pizzas and a bag of Doritos is less than a pound and a half of food. Less than. Trust me, I've weighed it a thousand times."

The woman took the lid off the Tupperware container and stood. "After I'm done I'll weigh it all up and I'll bet you anything it weighs over two pounds. Just watch and see."

The woman pointed two fingers at Clint like a gun and then she turned them on herself and shoved them down her throat.

Clint turned and walked away as the violent gagging began.

The Rottweiler was waiting in the hallway.

FOUR

GREED

For what shall it profit a man, if he gain the whole world, and suffer the loss of his soul?
~Jesus Christ

Chapter Thirteen
Live Young

MOST ROACHES ARE oviparous. Their young grow in eggs outside of the mother's body. In these species, the mother roach carries her eggs around in a sac called an ootheca, which is attached to her abdomen. The number of eggs in each ootheca varies from species to species. Many female roaches drop or hide their ootheca shortly before the eggs are ready to hatch. Others continue to carry the hatching eggs and care for their young after they are born. But, regardless of how long the mother and her eggs stay together, the ootheca has to stay moist in order for the eggs to develop.

Other roaches are ovoviviparous. Rather than growing in an ootheca outside of the mother's body, the roaches grow in an ootheca inside the mother's body. In a few species, the eggs grow inside the mother's uterus without being surrounded by an ootheca. The developing roaches inside feed on the eggs' yolks, just as they would if the eggs were outside the body. One species is viviparous. Its young develop in fluid in the mother's uterus the way most mammals do.

They Don't Check Out

Ovoviviparous and viviparous species give birth to live young.

The number of young that one roach can bear also varies considerably. A German cockroach and her young can produce 300,000 or more roaches in one year. An American cockroach and her young can produce a comparatively small 800 new roaches per year.

Whether mother roaches care for their young also varies from one species to another. Some mothers care for their offspring after birth, and scientists believe that some offspring have the ability to recognize their mothers. Other mothers hide or bury their ootheca and never see their offspring and would not recognize them if they did.

Chapter Fourteen
Memories Come

CLINT WALKED UP to the winding stairs and the boy was sitting on the bottom steps waiting for him. His face was still bruised, but he looked different.

Younger.

Clint remembered him as being on the cusp of manhood, but apparently his memory had failed him. The boy couldn't be a day over ten with the last vestiges of baby fat still clinging to his cheeks.

"Is that your dog?"

Clint glanced down at the Rottweiler and said, "I guess so. You still waiting to go back home?"

"Yeah."

Clint sat next to the boy and the Rottweiler lay down at their feet. "It's not safe for you here," Clint said. "I realize that now very clearly."

"I know," the boy said.

"When I'm done here, I'm taking you with me. Maybe that's one of the reasons I came here. You think?"

The boy shrugged.

"It's strange," Clint said. "The people here . . . it's like they don't even realize they're trapped. It's almost like they are lost in their own minds or afraid to remember."

The boy stared at Clint solemnly and said, "The memories will come. You can only hide from them for so long."

Clint stood and said, "Good. They need to own all of it and if need be, I'll help them remember."

Clint put his hand on his satchel and mentally promised that he'd show them the way, one twisted mother fucker at a time. He'd help them remember if that meant crushing their skulls and letting the memories flow out. "You stay here and wait for me, okay?"

Clint pointed at the Rottweiler and commanded, "Stay."

The dog whined but remained compliantly still.

Clint turned to the boy and said, "He'll guard you until I get back."

The boy shrugged.

Clint walked up the stairs.

Chapter Fifteen
Depressive

CLINT STEPPED OFF the pink stairway and onto the obsidian floor. He stared at the staircase and waited for the walls to close in and seal the opening.

Nothing changed.

Clint turned away and felt a chill—like ghostly fingers tickling his spine and cold breath on his neck. He glanced back and the stairway was gone; he was trapped on the third floor. *Fine*, he thought, and he let the blood lust propel him further. If need be, he'd kill all of the occupants until he could finally get out of the accursed place.

The hallway was silent and empty except for several brown boxes stacked in front of a door down the left hallway. Clint strolled over and realized he was standing in front of Apartment 9. There were about a dozen boxes that seemed to have been mail ordered; Clint speculated it must be the resident's birthday.

Clint knocked on the door and waited for several minutes and then he let himself inside. The kitchen counters were covered with appliances: blenders, juicers, toasters, and mixers. There were several appliances Clint didn't recognize, and they were stacked so closely that they must have been unusable. Judging from their pristine appearance, the appliances were brand new and Clint refined his earlier speculation and decided the resident must have recently been married and the kitchen was far too small to house what must have been a major haul of wedding gifts. Clint opened a cabinet and saw it was filled with more appliances that were still boxed. Clint shuffled through the kitchen and realized all of the cabinets and the pantry were similarly filled.

There was no food.

"Bug Man," someone murmured.

Clint stepped into the living room and saw a woman with unkempt hair sitting on a lime green couch, her eyes glued to a television. The woman wore a long pink bathrobe and blank expression.

"Ma'am," Clint said, but she did not move and her gaze was unwavering.

The living room was so filled with boxes and stacks of newspapers that it looked like a makeshift maze with a pathway to the couch and then out to the bathroom and back bedrooms.

A hoarder.

Clint occasionally saw tenants living under less extreme conditions, but he had come to recognize the condition.

The volume was turned down and she was fixated on the Home Shopping Network. Two women were pimping out flameless candles—six of them for $14.95. The woman reached out, her eyes never leaving the television, picked up a cordless phone, dialed a number, and said, "I'd like to order the Luminera."

Clint recognized here voice—even though it lacked inflection. It was a whisper from decades gone.

He stared at her face and studied its contours. Her cheeks were slack and her eyes were heavily lidded, but Clint could see it. A face he last saw when he was seven and she was positioned within a coffin.

"Mother?" Clint asked.

She put down the receiver and continued to stare at the television.

It was obviously a cruel joke. Clint had pushed too hard and now the asylum was pushing back.

Clint turned away. As he entered the kitchen he felt a ghostly breath in his ear as she said, "I'll take two more."

The next apartment door was uncluttered by boxes and Clint wondered what apparition the asylum had dredged up for him within the room. His father was still alive, probably piss drunk at a biker bar, and he had no other departed relatives that he gave a shit about.

He knocked on the door and wondered if his departed grandmother, who spent her last years addled with Alzheimer's, was sitting in a rocking chair in the living room. Clint's most vivid memory of her was when she called him "little asshole" and slapped him across the head with a house shoe.

There was no answer.

Clint let himself inside and was relieved to find that the kitchen was uncluttered. He ducked around the corner and glanced into the living room.

Empty.

He silently unzipped the satchel and withdrew the 1911. The apartment might be empty or some ghostly presence might be hidden behind the shower curtain in the bathroom or crouched in the closet. I hope so, Clint thought. Send them straight to hell.

He walked quietly with the gun extended in front of him. He had no more patience for talk or speculation. The asylum tested him with the last room and Clint received the message. If he was here to lay down God's vengeance, then so be it.

Clint heard a soft sound coming from the back of the apartment—if the layout held true then it was a bedroom.

He listened and decided it was crying.

A woman or perhaps a child.

The boy?

Clint lowered the 1911 to his side and shouted, "Hello?"

The crying persisted, a steady whimpering occasionally broken by deep sobs and finally a faint whisper. "Bug Man."

Clint entered a dark bedroom and saw a woman curled up under a sheet that was pulled to her chin. As he neared her, he saw two prescription bottles sitting on a bedside table: Prozac and Lithium.

Clint stared down at her and asked, "Mom?"

She continued to cry softly.

"I didn't know you were on drugs," Clint said. "What is that stuff for, depression?"

She was unresponsive.

Not just depression, Clint thought. You don't piggyback Prozac and Lithium unless the condition is more severe than that. Hell, Jenn had been on Lexapro for as long as he'd known her and she was fine. Wasn't everyone at least a little depressive? Didn't everyone suffer in their own way? Bipolar? He considered the room down the hall where she sat surrounded by boxes she hadn't bothered to open. Newspapers she had never bothered to read. Hoarding things to ease some pain she couldn't touch.

Clint didn't remember her like that. Clint's memories of her were vague, but romanticized by time and loss. He remembered the way she held him in her lap and played with his hair. He remembered the song she sang to him as he fell asleep. "You Are My Sunshine."

Sunshine.

Clint remembered the way she looked in that coffin, all of the emotion erased from her face.

"Momma?"

His dad never explained how she had died. Clint glanced at the pill bottles and a dark thought intruded.

"Momma?"

Clint knelt and put his cheek down on hers. It was wet and warm, and her hair smelled sweet, like honey. "Mommy," he whispered. "Why can't you hear me?"

She reached out and pulled him in close and gently stroked his hair while she wept.

They stayed like that for a while and finally she withdrew and rolled over on her side.

Clint stood and slowly walked out of the bedroom, through the living room, into the kitchen, and out of the apartment. She was so young—younger than he was now.

So young.

Chapter Sixteen
Sick Game

CLINT WALKED AWAY from the apartment and saw the boy sitting on the staircase. The same boy, only younger, that much was undeniable now. The white T-shirt hung on the boy like an oversized football jersey and the baseball cap swallowed his head. A border collie sat at the boy's feet and stared up at Clint with soft eyes.

"Did you see her?" the boy asked, his voice fragile and distant.

"I did," Clint said. "What's waiting for me in the other apartments on this floor? Is my mom in all of them?"

The boy shrugged.

Clint couldn't verbalize the thoughts that echoed in his mind. Was she committing suicide further down the hallway? Was she somewhere down there waiting in a coffin? "I'm not going into those other apartments. No way."

The boy studied Clint's face and asked, "You understand now, don't you?"

"Understand what?" Clint asked.

"Memories," the boy said. "The further you go, the more important the memories. It wants you to remember."

"Who?" Clint shouted, fueled by a sudden surge of anger.

The boy sighed and said, "The asylum. It wants you to remember."

"That's bullshit. I remember everything. There's a difference between trying not to remember and focusing on what's important. I have a wife at home waiting on me. That's what is true. This . . . it's just a sick game," Clint screamed, his voice echoing down the hallway. The border collie gently whined. "The asylum is fucking with me. Pushing me. I get it though. I understand the rules."

"Do you?"

"Sure," Clint insisted. "I'll go on—march right up these fucking stairs and take all of the punches this place can throw at me. But you know what? I'm going to throw my own punches as well. I'm here with a purpose. This place can't dissuade me."

"Okay," the boy said and he shrunk away from Clint and the baseball cap fell down over his face. "You're just stirring up a hornet's nest."

Clint knelt down and said, "You know I'm not mad at you, right?"

The boy shrugged.

"I'll get us out of here," Clint promised. "I will."

"I hope so," the boy said softly.

"I will," Clint said and he stepped over the border collie and moved up the stairs.

FIVE

HERESY

Suffering becomes beautiful when anyone bears great calamities with cheerfulness, not through insensibility but through greatness of mind.

~*Aristotle*

Chapter Seventeen
Incendiary

CLINT STORMED UP to Apartment 13. In the middle of the door was a brass knocker shaped like a plump cherub who flew up and then dropped down to kiss its twin each time he banged it.

He heard movement within and sensed an eye studying him through the keyhole. He rapped the knob again and noticed the cherubs were wild-eyed with fear.

Fly away. Kiss. Fly away. Kiss.

He stepped back from the door so that he could be clearly seen through the keyhole. "Anyone home? This is the Bug Man. Southeastern Pest Control."

No response.

Clint unlocked the door and tried to open it, but it was held tight by a thin chain.

"Pest Control," he yelled into the crack.

"Go away," ordered a gravelly voice behind the door.

"I won't be but a moment, sir."

Clint could see a form move into the space revealed by

the thin crack. It was a small man bundled up in a white blanket, with a pale face and dark sunglasses like those a blind man would wear. "Is anyone else out there?"

Clint scanned the hallway, but it was empty. "Nope."

The door closed and he heard the chain being unfastened. The figure within said, "You mean no one that you can see." The door opened and Clint got a good look at the tenant. "Just because you can't see them doesn't mean they aren't there."

The man stepped out of the kitchen and disappeared around the corner. The impression he was wrapped in a white sheet was correct and he was wearing dark shades, but Clint was wrong about his face. What he mistook as pale skin was actually thin, white medical bandages carefully wrapped around his entire face, leaving only tiny nostril holes and a dark slit at his mouth. He resembled a freshly wrapped mummy, or the invisible man. Clint wondered if there was anything of substance beneath the sheet and the bandages. Clint also wondered if he was best off killing the man now, or hearing out his demented history first. Better to go with the flow—the boy had told him that.

Clint stepped inside and surveyed his surroundings, and to the tenant's credit, the kitchen was immaculate, and there was a strong scent of bleach and artificial lemon cleaner. Clint opened the cabinets and everything was neat and tidy; in fact, the cans of vegetables appeared to have been arranged alphabetically. Clint sprayed under the refrigerator and moved into the living room. The pale-faced man was sitting in a plush easy chair that threatened to swallow him.

"If you don't mind me asking," Clint began, "what were you worried about out there?"

"Pardon?" With effort, he squiggled out of the chair like a butterfly stretching its way out of a cocoon.

"You asked me if anyone was out there," Clint said. "What are you afraid of?"

"The past."

Clint frowned and said, "I don't understand."

"True. You would think that we could put the past behind us. Some do, I've heard, and good for them. Of course, most of us cannot. Most of us become the very thing we despise the most."

"What have you become?"

"A victim. *You* wouldn't know about that condition though."

Clint nodded.

"But you will."

"I'll take your word for that. Listen—"

"Your timing is dead on," the pale faced man interrupted. "It's just about time to feed. Would you like to stay a bit?"

The mention of eating brought sudden attention to the fact that he was starving. "Sure. Thanks for the offer."

They walked into the dining room. There was a round oak table with three chairs placed around it and in the center sat a bowl filled with plastic fruit. "Make yourself comfortable," the bandaged man said politely. "I'll be right back." He moved into the kitchen and shuffled around in the pantry closet. A moment later he returned holding a large Tupperware bowl.

Clint recoiled.

His hands were covered in soft, oversized gloves. He sat down in front of Clint and pulled his chair in close so that the bowl was placed directly in front of both of them. Several small holes had been poked into the lid as if to let whatever was hidden within breath.

"What's in there?"

He didn't answer. Instead, he unwrapped the bandages from his face. Like rice shaken out of a bridal veil, bits of white fell away from the spaces within the bandages and landed on the table. Unlike rice, these bits wiggled and squirmed—angered that they were shaken out of their hiding places within the inner layers of wrappings. Little by little, his face came into view and then, saving the best for last, he removed his sunglasses.

Clint gasped.

"It really is horrid. I do apologize."

Clint fought past his revulsion and wondered if the man standing in front of him was a corpse. How could this twisted thing be anything else?

"What happened to you?"

"I told you what I've become. Few people with burns as severe as mine even live." His entire face and neck were a mass of angry scar tissue. Most of his flesh was charred black with traces of red so vivid it seemed to pulse. Here and there were patches of fragile pink skin seemingly out of place amidst the thick scabs and consuming darkness. "This is the best part of me. The rest is far worse."

He motioned as if to open the sheet.

"No. Please don't."

"If you insist."

His lidless eyes were wet gleaming orbs that served to remind Clint that the monstrosity in front of him was still alive. Tears rolled down his cheeks and were lost within the cracks littering his face.

Clint allowed himself to see more and the true horror came into focus. Within the crevices and scabs of his ruined flesh were countless squirming maggots contentedly feeding.

Clint turned away from him and tried not to be sick. His hand fell to the satchel and he wondered if his purpose here was to deliver a mercy killing. "I'm sorry," Clint mumbled.

"No, not at all," he said. "I'm disgusting. How could I deny it?"

Clint steeled himself and turned back to face the monstrosity. His ruined face was frozen into a permanent scream. His lips and most of his cheeks had been burned away and most of his chin had melted into his throat.

"Did someone do that to you?"

"No. Not the first time, anyway. That one belongs to me and I won't deny it. I was causing mischief one night and finally my antics caught up to me. Embarrassing, really. You would think an incendiary would know better, but I was very enthralled by my work, expanding the boundaries."

"Incendiary?"

"Yes, perhaps you would call me a pyromaniac or . . . of course, look who I'm speaking to." He laughed. "A firebug. I'm what *you* would call a firebug. I was so eager to see the fruits of my labor that I got a good taste of my own medicine. It's one thing to wait outside and listen to the screams, but I wanted to watch." He reached up with a white, gloved hand and briefly shielded his wet eyeballs. "The light hurts my eyes. What I'd give to just be able to blink. Of course, the good news is I sleep with two eyes open, a necessity around here."

"You tried to burn people?"

"Tried? Come, come. On that night, I ventured too close and the roof in the nursery collapsed. Poetic justice, you might say. I was in a medically induced coma for two months with fifth degree burns over eighty-five percent of my body, a near fatal infection, and kidney failure. Apparently, I was given a five percent chance to live."

"Well, did you?" Clint asked.

"What?" He laughed. "Not nice. You're so bad. Do you know my butt was completely burned flat? They had to amputate most of my toes, and my hands are about as useful as the hooks on an unlucky pirate. The burns went through all the layers of my skin, down into muscle and bone and, between you and me, even deeper. Not that I'm complaining, job hazard and all that. Still it was long ago. Water under the bridge."

"Some of your wounds look fresh to me."

"True. It loves to pick at old wounds. That's part of the process. I am never allowed to forget." He opened the Tupperware bowl and Clint could see movement within. "Speaking of picking at old wounds, it's feeding time."

He reached into the bowl and withdrew a handful of writhing maggots, like the ones that fell out of his wrappings earlier. Carefully, one by one, he placed the ravenous creatures on his face and after a bit of squirming they settled in to their duties.

"You're fucked up," Clint said, rising up from the table.

He laughed. "They're helping me. Clearing away the dead skin and making way for the new." His voice grew serious, "Of course, it really is pointless. Once I begin to look human again it will just come for me and take it away. *Que sera, sera*. Before you leave, would you mind helping me with the fresh wrappings?"

Clint stood and considered the 1911 nestled in his satchel. One bullet and the burned man would be gone. Instead, Clint turned and walked out of the apartment and into the hallway.

Some people don't deserve mercy.

Chapter Eighteen
Avoidance

CLINT STOOD IN front of Apartment 14 and wondered what sort of monstrosity could be living next to the burned man.

Stir up the hornet's nest?

Damn right.

Clint took the 1911 out of the satchel and rapped on the door with the butt of the gun.

A moment later the door opened and an elderly gentleman wearing a tan blazer and a baby blue tie asked, "Do we have an appointment?"

Clint held the gun at his side and said, "We do."

"Fair enough. Come on in." The old man had a gentle, familiar face, like a lost grandfather he glimpsed in black and white photographs long ago and almost forgotten. They stepped into the kitchen and Clint closed the door behind them. "Would you like some tea? I have green, white, oolong, herbal . . . "

"No, thanks."

The man wore thick glasses and his enlarged eyes stared deep into Clint's eyes. After a few long seconds he asked, "Are you feeling all right?"

Clint blinked and said, "Sure, I am."

"Could I offer you an espresso?" He walked up to a silver espresso machine and opened a cabinet above it that was filled with small coffee cups.

"No, thanks." Clint wanted a drink, but it sure as fuck wasn't tea or coffee. He could feel the soothing buzz slowly receding toward a dull headache. Clint tucked the 1911 back into his satchel. The man walked into the living room and Clint quickly sprayed around a pristine kitchen and a closet pantry that was empty except for a box of Godiva Gourmet Biscuits.

"Don't bother, Bug Man," he said from the living room. "I keep my office as clean as a whistle."

"Office?" Clint stepped into what he had assumed was the living space, but instead it was arranged like a therapist's office. A leather couch and two plush chairs were centered around a coffee table. A desk and surrounding bookshelf were set against a far wall, and a dry erase board was mounted on the other. Soft light emanated from several standing lamps with pastel shades. A potted palm tree filled up a lonely corner. A painting of a laughing Buddha was mounted next to an ornate wooden cross.

Clint's eyes settled on this apparent paradox and the old man laughed and said, "I'm an atheist, but I value everyone's beliefs."

Clint walked around the room, spraying Deltamethrine after each step and paused at the desk. A diploma mounted on the wall established that Frederick M. Gastineaux obtained a PhD. in Clinical Psychology from Texas A&M. The bookshelf held dozens of medical journals and novels with provocative titles such as: *The Sociopath Next Door*; *Stumbling on Happiness*; *Games People Play*; *Memories, Dreams, Reflection*; and *The Divine Comedy*.

"Come sit down and get comfortable." Dr. Gastineaux sat in the middle of the leather couch and gestured across the coffee table at one of the plush chairs.

Clint considered the offer. The tank on his back was heavy and his legs felt weak. "Okay." Clint unstrapped the tank and settled into the chair. It was oversized, and as he stared across at the doctor, he felt like a child held in the thrall of authority.

The doctor picked up a notebook pad and a pen and though his expression was kind, his eyes reflected disappointment as he asked, "Can I be perfectly frank with you?"

"Sure."

"Good. Have you been drinking?"

Clint took a deep breath and said, "A little bit."

"Hmmm, hmmm." The doctor scribbled something in the notebook and asked, "And what do you call a little bit?"

"I had a few drinks with . . . just a few drinks."

"A few?"

Clint sank deeper into the chair and said, "A few. Listen, I don't typically drink on the job. Never."

"Never?"

Clint laughed nervously. "Listen, I really don't. It's not something I'm proud of. Not something I'd tell anyone. I'm naturally a secretive person. You asked me, so I told you."

"It's not something I'd repeat," the doctor said reassuringly. "Anything you tell me stays here. You know that."

"Good," Clint said. "It's been a rough day."

"How so?" The doctor leaned in, almost imperceptibly, as if held in rapt attention.

Clint stared across at him and mentally retraced his day and suddenly realized the old bastard was mind fucking him. He hadn't come here as a patient. He was the professional and this guy his client. If anyone was going to be asking questions, it was Clint. "What are you, like a therapist?"

The doctor leaned back and said, "I'm a clinical psychologist. You are perhaps thinking of a counseling psychologist. My specialty is less general and more focused on individuals with serious mental illness."

Clint laughed and said, "Then you chose an interesting place to live. You know this place used to be an asylum, right?"

"A Behavioral Health Center. I don't just live here, this is also where I see patients."

"Patients?" Clint asked. "Kind of a distance to make them come, isn't it?"

"Not at all. My patients all live here."

Clint considered the other tenants and nodded in agreement. "I could see that. Do you treat that freak next door?"

The doctor frowned and said, "I'm not at liberty to discuss my other patients."

"Other?" Clint asked incredulously. "I think there's been a misunderstanding, buddy. I'm not a patient, I'm the—"

"Bug Man?"

"Yeah," Clint agreed. "The technical term is pest control technician or, if you prefer, exterminator."

"I see," the doctor nodded and quickly scribbled in his notebook.

Clint stood and strapped the tank to his back and said, "I'll get out of your hair."

The doctor remained seated and said, "Allow me to provide a brief biography that might gain me a bit of credibility. You see, I myself suffer from paranoid schizophrenia. I use the present tense because though I no longer deal with constant delusions, I am acutely aware there is not a permanent cure for my illness."

"Okay," Clint said, cognizant that despite the framed diploma and bookshelf filled with medical journals, this guy was just as nutty as the rest of the tenants.

"Research suggests the disease is caused by a viral infection during the second trimester of pregnancy." The doctor laughed and said, "As is so often the case you could blame this one on the mother. My schizophrenia didn't fully manifest until I was in my mid-twenties. At the time, I was active in the military guarding atomic weapons. I developed a debilitating paranoia that my fellow marines were secretly agents from enemy nations intent on taking over all of the nuclear installations in one fell swoop. I was soon discharged though, at the time, my disease remained undiagnosed.

"Almost a year later I stumbled into a Wal-Mart fully believing that I was an atomic bomb equipped with an internal mechanism set to detonate. I believed the detonation trigger was a phrase that some stranger would utter to me at the appropriate time. I physically assaulted a wheelchair-bound greeter and was thrown into a maximum security mental hospital cell."

"Okay," Clint said, certain he knew which mental hospital.

The doctor smiled and said, "That could have been the end of my story, but it wasn't." He reached into the inside pocket of his blazer and pulled out a prescription bottle. "Here," he said as he tossed the bottle to Clint. Clint caught it and saw that it was labeled Risperdal. "You keep these," the doctor urged. "I've got plenty."

Clint put them in his satchel.

The doctor scribbled in his notebook and tore the page out. He folded it over, stood, and handed it to Clint. "The medication alone isn't enough of course. It takes constant psychotherapy and, above all else, avoidance."

Clint shoved the paper in his front pocket and asked, "Avoidance?"

"Absolutely," the doctor agreed. "I have to avoid people, places, and hostile environments where I might be stressed. Stress, you see, is the ultimate trigger. I've even had to teach my friends and family members to avoid statements that might be interpreted as accusations and how to avoid otherwise agitating me. Drugs and alcohol are, of course, off limits and even nicotine can be a potential trigger."

"That must suck," Clint said.

The doctor shook his head and said, "No, what sucks is being under the thrall of delusion."

"Do you want me to spray the back?" Clint asked.

The doctor considered and said, "Could you spray the closet in the back room?"

"Okay," Clint said. He walked into the hallway and

stepped into an empty room that was dark except for a trickle of light that crawled in and died halfway inside.

Clint stepped into the blackness and felt for the closet door. The handle was cold and unfriendly. Clint opened the door and pointed his rod at the space he knew to be the closet and as his finger settled on the trigger he was shoved from behind and he fell against the back wall of the closet.

The door behind him closed.

"What the fuck?" Clint shouted and he scrambled to his feet and felt for the doorknob.

It was locked from the outside.

"This is called exposure therapy."

"Fuck you," Clint screamed. "I'm going to break your fucking hip."

"This is for your own good."

Clint felt around the closet and thankfully it was empty, but it was also shockingly narrow. His shoulders grazed the side walls. The tank of Deltamethrine pressed against the back wall.

Clint was packed in too tightly to kick the door with any real force.

Breathe, Clint told himself. Breathe.

The darkness was absolute.

Clint beat on the door with clenched fists, but with no leverage it was pointless.

Memories.

He used to shove Clint in here after Mommy died. Sometimes for hours, but more often all night.

Clint reached into the satchel for the 1911 and his fingers fell on a prescription bottle. He unconsciously fumbled with the lid as if in the thrall of muscle memory and brought two pills up to his mouth. Clint swallowed them dry and the taste was repulsively bitter.

The closet door creaked open.

Clint pulled the 1911 out of the satchel and kicked the door open.

The dark room was empty.

Clint rushed through the hallway with the 1911 extended in front of him and sprang into the living room.

It was barren. Not only was the doctor gone, but the furnishings were somehow gone as well. White walls, barred windows, and nothing else. Clint walked into the kitchen and it was also empty except for a lonely teapot that sat on the stove.

Clint looked down at his hands and saw the 1911 gripped in his right and in his left he held a prescription bottle of Risperdal.

Chapter Nineteen
Home Sweet Home

CLINT CASUALLY STRODE down the hall and up to the next apartment. His headache had receded to a dull, distant throb and the horror of his predicament seemed abstract and distant. Clint was simply an observer of misery and none of it his own. Risperdal. Clint had been taking it, on and off, for most of his adult life. How had he forgotten? How had he forgotten about his schizophrenia? Could all of the crazy shit that had been happening to him be an extreme relapse?

If so, then he would be okay now, the Risperdal was designed to kick in quickly. No more delusions.

The apartment was unnumbered. Clint banged his fist against the brown oak door and it opened.

Clint gasped.

It was his living room. There was no doubt. He could plainly see the gray couch that was a holdover from his single days, the green easy chair they had bought on layaway at Ashley Furniture, the flat screen Sony television mounted on the wall, the antique bookshelf Jenn had purchased from a little shop downtown, and the flowery rug and the photographs.

"Jenn," he shouted, hoping beyond hope that he had found a way home and this wasn't just another cruel trick.

Silence.

Clint closed the door behind him and stared at a framed

photograph on the wall of he and his wife curled up in a hospital bed. Jenn was pale and tired. A newborn child was wrapped in a blanket as tight as a burrito—eyes narrow and blue, face still red from the effort of being born. They held the child between them like a trophy.

Michael.

Memories came flooding in. Of course he had been born. Why hadn't he remembered? How could he have forgotten? Fourteen hours of intense labor and finally the doctors demanded a C-section when his pulse dropped too low.

A healthy son over nine pounds.

Jenn was afraid to hold him, fearful he might break. Two days later she took him, but she refused to breastfeed. Besides, he had already acclimated to the bottles the nurses fed him every two hours. On the fourth day they brought him home.

The tank felt heavier as Clint stepped out of the living room and into the nursery. The silence followed.

Clint remembered stumbling inside the nursery, night after night, after hours of watching his train set while the whiskey flowed freely. Michael was less than three weeks old then and Clint recalled staring down at his son on those drukcn nights, crying silently.

Jenn had withdrawn completely. They called it postpartum depression. The baby blues. She had become robotic since the birth. Perhaps long before. She fed the baby at arm's length and for Clint the distance was even greater.

The doctors said it would only last a few weeks.

Clint remembered all of this as he stared at an empty crib and then his memories pushed further, insistent now.

A bathtub.

No. He would not remember all of it. Could not.

Clint left the ursery and walked into their bedroom and stared at the bed. A body pillow, almost the length of a body, divided it perfectly in half.

The silence was broken by a drip. It came from the

adjoining bathroom. The bathtub faucet had always leaked and hadn't he promised to fix it?

"I don't want to remember," Clint said aloud. Any sound to interrupt the monotonous dripping.

Jenn never asked him for help and God knows he would have tried. How do you help someone who is lost so deeply within their own pain that they've embraced it? Formed a body around it and fed it until nothing else remains.

Clint stepped into the bathroom.

The bathtub was empty, but it wasn't always so.

A water droplet, like memories, collected at the rim of the faucet until it became too heavy and fell.

Memory.

Clint stumbled into the house, careful not to wake silent, sullen, withdrawn Jenn. Mentally, spiritually, and physically withdrawn. That last part he would be working on soon. His aunt had agreed to watch Michael tomorrow night and he would take her out to Auntie Pasta's for fettuccine and Italian margaritas and hold her hand and pull out her chair and start the whole courting process from scratch if he had too. Would he settle for a kiss at the end of the night? Certainly, if that's all she had to give.

The bedroom was dark, but Clint knowingly avoided the chest of drawers and the standing fan as he blindly navigated his way toward his side of the bed. He stripped as silently as possible until he was naked, except for his tube socks. He sat at the edge of the bed and reached down for his feet and the room began to spin. He put a foot on the ground to anchor himself and slowly counted to twenty. The room stopped. He could make out the outline of her body. He reached out to put a hand around her waist. She was too soft, and he realized it was the body pillow.

She was gone.

"Jenn?" he asked softly.

Silence except for the dripping that echoed from the bathroom.

"Jenn." This time louder.

Clint slowly worked his way back to his feet.

He pulled back the blinds and confirmed that his truck and her minivan were still parked side by side in the driveway. Thank God, she hadn't left him yet. He still had time to get his shit together. And he would get it together, beg her for forgiveness again, and work toward another sobriety chip.

One day at a time.

The digital clock glowed in the darkness: 1:28 a.m. The fan gently whirred, but above it all was the steady dripping. Clint went to the bathroom door—a faint light shone beneath the door.

"Jenn."

Clint opened the door.

A candle burned next to the sink.

Jenn was sprawled out in the bathtub, asleep.

The water had been drawn up to the edge of the tub—just beneath her chin.

"Jenn?"

Her eyes remained closed and she did not stir.

The water was dark and thick.

Clint fumbled for the light switch and the water turned red.

Jenn was pale and lifeless.

Clint fell to his knees and crawled toward the bathtub.

"No."

Clint reached into the murky water and pulled out her arm. Her wrist had been sliced almost to the bone. Her arm was cold.

"No."

Michael? Clint reached down into the water and blindly fumbled around between her legs and he felt it then.

Jenn was not alone.

Clint stared at the empty bathtub and remembered.

Memories will come, the boy said.

They Don't Check Out

Clint felt the weight of it.

Clint stumbled out of his bathroom, through his bedroom and the living room, and back out into the hallway. It was only as he closed the door to his past that he realized he was weeping.

Chapter Twenty
Roach Motel

THE ASYLUM WAS not unlike the archaic roach traps that were popular in the '70s. Roach motels they had been called. It lured the mindless insects into a miniature labyrinth with the promise of sustenance and once they forced themselves inside, they were poisoned and left to slowly die and decay. A cheerful motto: They Check In, But They Don't Check Out.

Amusing.

Staircases that led upward and closed behind their unwitting prey. Barred windows. A persistent hope of some unreachable goal. And wasn't life just like that?

Clint adjusted the straps of his backpack. It should have grown lighter as he let loose the streams of poison, but the weight of it only grew. An endless supply of poison.

Somewhere beneath him was a ceiling that dripped blood on a mattress beneath it and a butterfly stain that seemed to flutter, yet was trapped within.

Jenn? He tried to toss the thought aside, but he could not. He tried to blame her for what she had done to herself. To Michael. He tried to hate her, but how can you hate someone you have spent so much time trying to love?

It was far easier to blame himself.

Clint hoped that the horrors he was facing were simply a manifestation of his own mind, his schizophrenia fully in control. They weren't. Clint took his medication and still they persisted.

Earlier, Clint embraced the notion that he was an innocent trapped in a hell created for the irredeemable. God's work. He could see now that he was wrong. Innocence is reserved for children.

The only innocent soul he had encountered in this accursed place was the boy. Clint thought of the sad boy and he felt a growing affection.

He loved the boy. Loved him.

Maybe, Clint thought, *I'm not irredeemable*. Maybe redemption was not out of reach. Maybe there was a purpose for him beyond suffering.

Clint closed his eyes, swept the pain aside, and promised he would save the boy. If he achieved nothing else, then that much he would do and, in doing so, maybe he could find something resembling peace.

Clint stared at the door that led to his house and realized if he chose he could step back inside and eventually he could forget. He could sit in the easy chair and watch television and occasionally glance at the family photograph and pretend his wife was asleep in the bedroom. Michael softly snoring in his crib. An endless supply of whiskey in the cabinet. A train that runs circles for eternity.

Memories fade.

Clint turned away and ran for the stairs, searching for the boy.

The stairs were covered with fresh blood.

The boy was gone.

A border collie lay at the foot of the stairs. The dog had been stabbed dozens of times and a pair of scissors was embedded in its shoulders—pushed down to the handle.

Clint screamed, and above, he heard an answering cry.

The boy.

SIX

VIOLENCE

To have a body is to suffer.

~*Bodhidhama*

Chapter Twenty-One
German Cannibals

SOME SPECIES OF cockroaches eat human eyelashes. In particular, they prefer to target babies, because their eyelashes contain important minerals and their tear ducts contain an ample supply of moisture. Also helpful is that babies are helpless to the onslaught.

The German cockroach is omnivorous and a scavenger. They particularly like starch, sugary foods, grease, and meats. In certain situations where there is a shortage of foodstuffs, they may eat household items such as soap, glue, and toothpaste, or they may even turn cannibalistic, often chewing on the wings and legs of each other.

Chapter Twenty-Two
Black Tears

THE FAMILIAR HALLWAY stretched out on either side of Clint, but a red marking on the wall diminished the sense of *déjà vu*.

A large swastika defaced the white wall, seemingly painted by a tentative, unskilled hand—a child's finger painting. It had almost certainly been painted with blood and, judging from the size of it, at least a gallon or more had been necessary. A pig's worth of blood if they squeezed the creature dry.

The symbol made Clint uneasy in the same way that a casual utterance of the words nigger and cunt caused an inward cringe of moral discomfort. It was a taboo that he preferred to ignore, but there it was as blatantly displayed as a prostitute soliciting in front of a church. It was a symbol that echoed Hitler and the holocaust in the faint way that history books and Hollywood creations are capable of, but Clint had seen it before in a much more intimate fashion.

Clint was twenty and he and a couple of friends, Big Dave and Little Sherm, were inner tubing down the Brazos River, each of them nestled in black tubes that fit them as tightly as life jackets. A fourth tube connected to Big Dave by a nylon rope held a Styrofoam cooler filled with Natural Lite.

It was a scalding summer day and the air was heavy and unrelenting, but the water somehow remained chilly and the beer went down cold and easy. Dozens of joyful strangers floated amidst them like ducks, anticipating the next gentle rapid that would usher them forward between long stretches of calm water. Clint enjoyed a peaceful buzz and behind his dark shades his eyes were closed. His biggest worry was how he was going to get a Marlboro and his lighter out of a Ziploc bag in the cooler without fumbling it into the water.

Clint heard Big Dave scream, "What the fuck?" and Clint opened his eyes and saw that a large raft had floated up next to them. Four men easily a decade older than Clint and his friends stood on the raft, two of them holding oars. It took Clint a moment to realize that one of them was pissing off the edge and the steady stream of urine was striking the side of Big Dave's inner tube and splashing onto him. Clint noted this and his eyes traveled up from the brazen penis and fixated on a black swastika tattooed across the man's broad chest. The man stared down at Big Dave dismissively and slowly shook his cock and tucked it back into a tight pair of blue jeans that had been cut into shorts that hung just above his knees.

Little Sherm frantically splashed away from the raft, but Big Dave was unaccustomed to such meekness. He was six feet, five inches tall and well over three hundred pounds. Only a bad knee prevented him from cashing in on a full-ride scholarship as an offensive lineman for the University of Texas. He was a gentle person and hard to provoke, but Clint had once seen him take a punch in the face from a fraternity punk and quickly reach out to choke him with one hand while delicately balancing his beer in the other.

Clint's first thought was that the situation might be avoided if it just didn't escalate when he heard Big Dave scream out an insult about the size of the man's penis that was quickly followed by a promise that he would fuck the man's mother. Clint's recollection of the events thereafter was hazy, as if a fog of rage had settled upon the river and obscured all but the most significant details.

The man with the "dick clit," as Big Dave described it,

went into a sort of rage Clint had only seen mimicked by professional wrestlers before an especially testosterone-fueled match. The man screamed and the words were incomprehensible, a lost guttural language, and veins and arteries appeared all over his muscular torso. His neck expanded until its edges seemed to extend beyond his ears, as if in his extreme anger his bald head might sink down into his chest.

Big Dave was particularly confined by his inner tube, yet he was inexplicably trying to reach up and pull himself into the raft. The men with oars were as shocked by the proceedings as Clint, but in a moment they would surely walk over to the edge of the raft and pummel Big Dave until his body went limp and casually floated downriver toward the next set of rapids.

Clint's eyes met those of one of the oarsmen and there was an instant understanding that they would fight. Like the primal equivalent of a middle school dance, Clint had been chosen. The man had long greasy hair, a wild beard, and several dark teardrops tattoos trailed down his cheeks.

"David," Clint screamed, and the sound of his name short-circuited his fight or flight response. "Let's get to the shore."

The shore was less than twenty yards away and Little Sherm was almost there already. Big Dave compliantly reached back with his long arms and swam the backstroke toward the shore. The bald Aryan screamed and flexed, and the oarsmen directed the raft toward Bid Dave. Clint feared that at any moment the Aryan might dive out of the raft and wrestle Big Dave out of his inner tube, but the four men were content to engage on the shore.

Clint reached the shore first and Little Sherm ran up to him and said, "Here," while handing him a thick branch that was at least two-feet long. Dave flipped out of his inner tube and stumbled ashore, much of the earlier bravado draining from his face.

The branch felt heavy and comforting in Clint's hands and he gripped it like a samurai sword. The raft was now only a few yards from the shore and the bald Aryan was as red as a boiled lobster.

Clint waved the branch in front of him and shouted, "I'm going to open up the skull of the first mother fucker that tries to climb out of that raft." Clint was fully aware that he held the tactical advantage of higher ground and wanted to make sure the Aryans knew it as well.

The oarsman with the beard said something Clint couldn't hear and then the raft slowly paddled away while the bald Aryan shouted obscenities.

Clint and his friends sat on the shore and drank a few beers and waited for their adrenaline to wear off. They talked about how close those four assholes had come to an ass whooping. None of them truly believed this, but they were unwilling to admit how scared they had been.

Terrified.

Thirty minutes after their near death experience, they were floating down the river again, beers in hand, tucked into their inner tubes like death row inmates who had narrowly escaped electrocution.

Clint was visualizing the teardrops that seemed to flow from black, unblinking eyes, when an inflatable duck paddled up next to him—a middle-aged man who wore a T-shirt to conceal a flabby belly and soft man breasts. "Are you the guys who got into that shit?"

"Huh?" Clint asked.

"Those fuckers in the raft. They are waiting for you a ways down where it gets shallow. I think one of them has a knife."

"What?" Big Dave asked.

The man shifted uneasily in his inner tube and said, "I think you guys are in big trouble. I swam back here to tell you. I saw what those punks did to you." The man paddled away and settled back next to a wide-eyed woman and a child who sat in a float shaped like a cartoon whale.

Little Sherm said, "Fuck it," and swam toward the shore.

Big Dave shook his head and somberly said, "I'm not going to hide from those fuckers. Eventually they are just going to come back here for us and then they will know we are chicken."

And with that statement, the line had been drawn and Clint knew he had to choose. Clint remembered a time during first grade when a bigger kid slapped him across the face for God knows why. The other kids laughed like it was some kind of inside joke. Clint cried and ran to a teacher and the heat of that slap returned at odd times—a phantom reminder of his cowardice and shame. No matter how many times he replayed it in his head and slapped that kid back and stomped on him and stabbed that fucker with scissors that had morphed from childproof plastic into threatening steel, it had happened and there's no changing things that happen.

"Fuck them," Clint said.

"Damn straight," Big Dave agreed. "I'll punch the bald one in the throat and crush his larynx. That might just dissuade the others. Don't fuck around, Clint. Throats and knees."

"Yeah," Clint said and he felt a handprint form on his right cheek.

Little Sherm watched them from the shore as they floated down the river. Some of the ducks were oblivious as they moved past, but others whispered and gestured at them as if signifying sad resignation.

Clint drank his beer, slammed another, and tried to dull a fear that had risen and ebbed and then returned. Clint visualized kicking the bearded oarsmen in the knee and watching the kneecap spin. Lifting him up by his mass of hair and digging a thumb into his eye as deep as it would go and turning to the others and shouting, "Who's next?"

Clint replayed that scene hundreds of times in the few minutes it took them to float toward the familiar raft. The river depth dropped to a few feet and the raft was perched on an outcropping of rocks.

Kick the knee and then lift him up by his hair and . . .

The four men were handcuffed and several policemen were escorting them toward the shore. As it turned out, the Brazos River was heavily scrutinized by the local police for situations such as this.

Big Dave laughed and Clint smiled, and after they went back and retrieved him, Little Sherm promised he had their back. "Way back," he was fond of saying as they repeated their tale to all of their friends.

That night Clint curled up in his sleeping bag and cried uncontrollably for hours.

The bloody swastika on the wall held a memory for Clint that brought back a rush of adrenaline he thought he left on that lazy river and a sudden heat to his cheek.

The asylum was trying its damnedest to break Clint, that much was clear. First, it tried to demean him by surrounding him with vivid examples of the darkest aspects of humanity, consistently lowering the bar. When that tactic was unsuccessful, the asylum made it personal, prying into his consciousness and revealing his most guarded secrets. Clint refused to lie down and die, and then the asylum responded by taking the boy. Now, the asylum had reached into Clint's past and was preying upon his deepest fear.

But, yet again, the asylum had underestimated him.

Clint had been deathly afraid of the Neo Nazis once upon a time, but that was when he was still young and long before he realized he had nothing left to lose. Clint welcomed the opportunity to confront the ghosts from his past and he would smile as he emptied his gun into them.

Chapter Twenty-Three
The Crucified Man

CLINT DECIDED TO move down the left-hand hallway first, already a well-established pattern. Clint took off the backpack and laid it against the wall. He stretched up on his toes and slowly rotated his shoulders and he felt his muscles loosen and he imagined he was growing taller and wider. His anger fueled him. Nourished him. Formed its own body that replaced the fragile emotional one that had thus far served him faithlessly.

The 1911 was cold and light in his hand and eager to voice Clint's hatred one metallic burst at a time.

The hallway was narrower than it had been by half at least, and if Clint stood in the middle and stretched out his arms he could just touch both sides with his fingertips.

The ceiling had hovered at least two yards above his head, but now he could touch it without fully extending his arm.

Clint had once been claustrophobic, but that was a lifetime ago.

Clint walked down the hallway and carefully listened for any sound which might betray the location of the boy. The first door he came to was unnumbered and open a few inches. Clint paused in front of it, and from within he could just make out the faint sound of whimpering.

Clint pushed open the door with the toe of his boot and stepped inside. A loose bulb flickered above him and revealed a kitchen in a severe state of demolition. All of the appliances had been removed—including the sink—and the cabinet door was stripped. The air was heavy with black smoke that gathered at the ceiling in mass, like angry clouds.

The whimpering grew louder.

Clint stepped into the living room and found the source of the smoke. A porcelain toilet sat in the middle of the room and a small fire burned within. A stack of wood comprised of broken cabinets, desks, and crown molding was arranged next to it.

Fecal matter was smeared on the walls, as if a pack of monkeys had escaped from captivity and was retaliating against the captors' abode.

The whimpering was coming from a back bedroom.

Clint moved deliberately and stepped quickly into the back hallway, glancing both ways lest some hostile force attack him. He was alone except, of course, for whoever was suffering in the bedroom.

Clint quickly opened the door and stepped inside with the 1911 extended in front of him.

Kermit Gosnell was crucified on the back wall.

Clint scanned the bedroom. In one corner was a pile of what appeared to be human excrement. *Why not,* Clint thought, *make a campfire in the toilet and shit where you sleep.* The walls were streaked with blood and feces—a Pollack original with a palette of brown and red. The elderly black man was nailed onto the wall—a grotesque performance art piece.

Clint imagined the art critics as they strolled up to him.

Clearly a Christ figure; about as subtle as a hammer to the head.

Hammer to the wrists, you mean, and right through the feet as well. The aesthetics and symmetry are surely diminished by the sheer number of nails. Six in his left foot, seven in his right.

Rusty nails and certainly too small to pass as authentic and certainly dressing him in a suit and tie is a strange choice.

Though it does seem to juxtapose materialism and the decay of—

I'd argue it's an ode to suffering—only modernized.

Sloppy work on his wrists and I'm certain Jesus wasn't nailed on at the shoulders and through the thighs as well.

A pair of men's underwear had been shoved into his mouth and deep into his throat. Kermit was wide-eyed and struggled to breathe through his blood-crusted nostrils.

Clint pulled out the underwear and Kermit gasped and glanced wildly around the room. "They are going to come back. Please get me down."

"Who?" Clint asked as he glanced back at the doorway.

Kermit fought past the pain and steadied his mind. "I don't know what they are. Some kind of feral things. They might have been human once—one of them still walks. My mom was a devout Christian and she used to warn me of heretics—I always imagined monsters."

"Aryans?"

"Yeah. Kind of. Please get me down. They're coming back. I think they want to . . . the woman said, 'Eat.' She said that."

"There's a woman with them?"

"Yes."

"Did you see a child?"

"No. Please get me down."

Clint glanced around the bedroom, his eyes always partially fixed on the doorway. Whatever hammer they had used to crucify Kermit was gone. "How do I get you down?"

Kermit struggled against the nails, but he was pinned as securely as a butterfly in a child's science project framed for posterity. Clint grabbed Kermit's right arm and pulled with all of his strength, and the nails seemed to shift deeper into his flesh. Kermit stifled a scream and his eyes rolled back and he managed to whisper, "Stop."

"What happened?" Clint asked.

"I don't know," Kermit said. "They broke into my

apartment and dragged me up the staircase. Something stirred them up. I heard other screams as well."

"I don't understand."

"Neither do I. It's the ones above. I've always known somehow that they were up there, but I thought I was safe from them. Somehow they . . . "

Kermit froze and his eyes locked on the doorway.

Clint heard it as well, a shuffling from the living room, coming closer. Clint quickly ran to the closet and opened the door. Empty. Clint stepped in and closed the door, leaving it open a crack, and waited. Kermit was wild-eyed with terror, silently pleading.

A moment later a woman crawled into the room.

She crawled low to the ground, haunches raised and elbows elevated like a small panther slowly stalking its prey. Her eyes were locked on the crucified man. She was naked, her body filthy with blood. Her wild hair was long and softly caressed the floor. A guttural moan escaped her throat.

Kermit bit down and stifled a scream as if a verbalization of his fear might spring her into some violent action. Or, perhaps he was afraid his screams might bring the others.

Clint watched as she slowly moved across the room and considered shooting her, but was fearful of what the gunshot might bring. What if the Aryans also had guns?

She moved past the closet and Clint realized she was small and fragile, with protruding ribs. She had lost any semblance of womanly curves.

She was wearing a wedding ring.

She slunk toward Kermit and paused in front of him.

She stared longingly up at his face.

"No," Kermit whispered.

She wrapped slender fingers around his ankles and slowly crawled up his body until she was standing on her tip toes. She slowly licked the blood away from his face, a mother cat cleaning her newborn.

She pulled away from him and said, "Eat."

They Don't Check Out

Kermit stared at the closet and hissed, "Kill her."

Clint leapt out of the closet and rushed her.

She turned toward Clint as his body slammed into her; the 1911 fell to the ground.

For a moment she was pinned between the two men. Clint grabbed her around the waist, lifted her into the air, surprised at how little she weighed, and slammed her to the cold floor.

She exhaled violently, the wind knocked out of her. Clint put his forearm against her fragile throat and pushed down with all of his weight.

She clawed at his arms and her fingernails dug into his flesh and etched deep, bloody grooves.

Clint was oblivious to the pain, oblivious as her windpipe collapsed, oblivious as she bit off her own tongue.

Clint stared through her, past her wild eyes, past her thrashing body, past the floor and into a room below, into a bathtub filled with blood, and further below where Michael was still waiting.

"She's dead."

Clint looked up. Kermit stared down at him. His eyes were wet.

The woman was still.

Clint picked up the 1911.

"Thank you," Kermit whispered.

"Okay."

"The others will come," Kermit said. "There's no way around it."

"I'll kill them too."

Kermit shook his head. "You don't have enough bullets for all of them. They aren't like her; they've been here much longer. You find a way out."

"I don't think I can get you down."

"I know."

Clint stared at Kermit and finally voiced what they were both thinking. "You want me to kill you?"

"Oh, God," Kermit whispered. "Please."

"Okay. I can't shoot you."

"I know."

Clint stared at the doorway—the others could come rushing in at any moment. Clint held the gun at his side and picked up the underwear.

Kermit nodded with understanding.

Clint shoved the underwear back into his mouth, careful to seal any opening where air might escape.

Kermit began to cry and Clint said, "Close your eyes."

He closed them.

Clint pinched his nostrils shut.

After a time his eyes flew open and stared at Clint, wet and unblinking.

Clint carefully pushed down his lids and said, "I'm sorry."

Clint turned away from the crucified man and slowly retraced his steps through the deserted apartment. There was nothing left now but to save the boy.

Chapter Twenty-Four
Feral Heretics

KISSING BUGS MIGHT conjure images of good things to come; however, this species of "true bugs" are not friendly. Kissing bugs are blood feeders that often partake of this activity while the victim is sleeping, biting where skin and plenty of blood is available, which often may be around the face. With their ability to bite and feed completely undetected, they are very successful in this lifestyle.

Humans are not their favorites though, as these insects prefer to feed on rodents, such as wood rats, but human blood appears to be a perfectly acceptable substitute.

The serious disease that can be spread to humans by kissing bugs is called Chagas disease. Of those infected, about 50,000 die from the disease each year. A number of domestic cases have occurred along the southern border of Texas, adjacent to Mexico.

Chagas disease can cause high fever, rashes, and a general fatigue, leaving victims unable to work. It is sometimes referred to as "American Sleeping Sickness," in reference to this symptom of a lack of energy and inability to function well.

The species called Triatoma infestans is particularly important in this disease cycle, for it appears to live almost exclusively within dwellings that house people. These insects, in the adult stage, have wings and are capable of flight;

however, in a home with food so close by they don't bother to fly, finding it most convenient and effective to walk from their hiding place to their blood meal. They are active only at night, when they emerge from hiding and begin waving their antennae around to pick up signals that will guide them to a sleeping person. Their antennae are extremely sensitive to three stimuli: odors, heat, and infrared light, the latter of which is given off by warm bodies. They are so tuned to feeding only on warm-blooded animals, they have been known to attempt to bite inanimate objects with the same temperature as bodies.

The insect injects some of its saliva as it begins to bite, and this acts as both an anesthetic to keep the victim from feeling the sharp proboscis entering the skin, and as an anticoagulant to keep the blood flowing properly. The insect feeds for several minutes, swelling from a flattened body to a bloated body, as it ingests several times its own weight in blood. The unfortunate part is that, in an effort to make more room in its body for more blood, it also defecates as it feeds, and within this excreted waste material there may be the protozoa that causes Chagas disease, a micro-organism called Trypanosoma cruzi. As the victim awakens and feels the sensation of the bite from the now long gone insect, there is a tendency to scratch at the spot of the bite, pushing some of the fecal matter and the pathogen into the skin and blood stream, thus starting the infection.

Assassin bugs live up to their name by jabbing their sharp mouths into other insects they've captured and sucking out the juicy stuff inside. In this effort, these insects certainly qualify as "beneficial" predators. Unfortunately, some of the different kinds are also given other names, and these are far more threatening to humans.

A person does not want to be bitten by these creatures, as their saliva can cause a variety of reactions, ranging from minor swelling and itching to potentially life-threatening allergic responses in sensitive people. The more often a person is bitten, the more severe a reaction, which could be as serious as swollen tongue, larynx and trachea, and difficulty in breathing. Some studies indicate that about seven percent of people may have a more serious reaction, even leading to anaphylactic shock that could come on immediately after the bite. Anyone who believes they have been bitten by an Assassin bug should seek medical help.

One kind, called the Masked Hunter, is a predator that feeds on bedbugs, and may be found indoors in homes where these insects are living. The bedbug has become a much more common problem in homes in North America, and this could increase the chances that the Masked Hunter will be present as well. This Assassin bug is not a blood feeder, but there could be an unfortunate encounter where someone's bitten. Assassin bugs often live in the nests of wild animals, such as wood rats or ground squirrels. They should be managed in some way if they appear near homes.

The mouth of an assassin bug is an amazing weapon, shaped like a stout, curved spike, that it plunges into the body of its victim. While not in use this "proboscis" is held beneath the body pointing backward, but once food is at hand, the insect extends it slightly forward and jabs its prey. The saliva of the insect feeder Assassin bugs is a mix of enzymes that dissolves the innards of other insects, and once liquefied, these tasty juices are then sucked out much the same way humans might enjoy a milkshake. Any parts that are left over are simply discarded. The saliva also has the ability to paralyze and immobilize the food prey, allowing the assassin bug to more thoroughly enjoy its meal without the need to hold on so tightly.

The narrow hallway was still and silent.

Clint quietly moved toward the next door. He put his ear

to the closed door, but no sound betrayed what was hidden within.

He turned the doorknob. Unlocked. He slowly pushed it open with his boot and cringed as the hinges creaked. He stepped inside and carefully closed the door behind him. The kitchen had been similarly demolished.

Silence.

He stepped into the living room. The floor was as caked with blood as a slaughterhouse and several bones littered the floor. The walls were finger painted with several swastikas and a massive Nazi flag hung against the back wall.

A section of the floor had been dug up and the boards and chunks of concrete were scattered around the room.

Clint walked over and stared down into the hole. He could see down into the apartment beneath.

The kitchen door creaked open.

Clint sprinted across the room and hid behind the billowy Nazi flag and watched as they moved into the room. Clint stared out at them through a small tear in the fabric, his eye fearful and unblinking.

The heretics were a strange juxtaposition of Aryan trailer trash and Maori warriors. They were lean and muscular and naked except they each wore tightly laced combat boots. Like the tribal people from New Zealand, they were completely covered in dark tattoos; however, there was no craftsmanship on display, only homemade tattoos etched with unsteady hands. Dark teardrops flowed from their eyes. Swastikas of varying shapes littered their bodies as well as skulls, grim reapers, and snarling demons. Words and phrases that conveyed prejudice and hatred. The black ink covered their heads and buttocks and even their dangling penises. The heretics were so covered with ink that they almost looked like living shadows with the darkness only broken by streaks of white that illuminated their hatred. There were six of them, and all but one moved on all fours as if they were raised by wolves, causing them to become feral.

The one man who stood upright seemed to be their leader. The others frequently glanced up at him for approval and cowered if he moved too close. His body was thick with muscle and when his mouth opened Clint could see his black tongue and gums and teeth that were filed into small daggers like a piranha. He spoke to the others in grunts and unfamiliar guttural phrases that came from deep within his throat.

Clint held the 1911 like a life preserver in turbulent waters and remained perfectly still. The feral heretics sniffed at the air as if searching for fear. One of them howled.

The leader raised a threatening hand that gripped a rusty hammer.

The howling stopped.

The leader stepped out of sight and a moment later there was a high-pitched scream.

Clint wondered how many he could kill before they overwhelmed him, and prepared to burst out and shoot the heretics. The screaming continued and Clint decided it wasn't the boy.

The leader moved back into the room, dragging the apartment manager behind him with a makeshift noose constructed of torn strips of sheets wrapped around his thick throat. The leader held the end of the sheet and effortlessly pulled Earl like an unruly dog on a leash.

"No," Earl screamed. "Please take the boy first. Take the boy."

The leader smiled, his teeth sharp and threatening, and in a deep voice he said, "Less meat."

Clint remained perfectly still and watched.

The feral heretics scurried over to Earl and held him firmly to the ground as he screamed and begged.

The leader reached down and ran his hand along Earl's remaining leg while the fat man squirmed. The leader's hand stopped at the thick calf and Earl fainted. The heretics laughed and the sound was as joyless as hyenas who have downed a gazelle and were ready to feed.

Feed.

Clint felt the true horror of the situation. The leader lifted the limp leg and opened his mouth.

Clint tossed the flag aside and fired at the leader, the bullet struck him in the shoulder and he dropped the hammer. The feral heretics scurried toward Clint with impossible speed.

Clint shot one in the chest from less than a yard away and the animal fell into a bloody heap. The first of them to reach Clint grabbed him by the legs and Clint pressed the muzzle of the gun into the top of his head and fired.

Before Clint could fire again the others were upon him.

Clint was jerked from his feet and the gun fell out of his hand and he hit the floor. They held Clint down, their fingernails digging into his flesh, and howled.

Clint glanced up and saw the leader standing above him.

Clint's gaze fixated on the tattoo of a child held in the grip of a skeletal grim reaper and the leader raised a boot above his face and stomped.

Clint felt his cheek shatter and heard a pop like a Black Cat on Independence Day. Clint noticed that Earl was awake and slowly crawling toward the front door. The leader followed his gaze, pointed, and the feral heretic who held Clint's right arm quickly scuttled toward Earl and pounced atop him.

Earl squealed and it elicited a primal response in the heretic because he bit down on Earl's thick shoulder and tore away a chunk of flesh.

This distracted the other heretics for a moment and they turned and stared longingly at the blood pouring out of the gory wound. Clint reached out for the 1911 that lay just within arm's reach and, with a surge of desperate energy, he grabbed the cold gun. The feral heretic grasping Clint's left arm never saw the gun as it came up to his temple.

Clint fired.

The heretic at Clint's feet tried to scramble up his body,

his teeth snapping rhythmically, but another bullet opened a small hole between his eyes.

As the body crumpled, Clint thought it wasn't so hard to kill someone.

The leader glanced around at his fallen kin, and then stared down at Clint and the gun, which was pointed at his groin. His testicles shrunk and his eyes grew wide.

Clint smiled, felt the pain in his shattered cheek, and he fired three times.

Not so hard at all.

Clint stood and saw that the last heretic was still trying to feed on Earl, while the fat man desperately squirmed beneath him. Clint felt *déjà vu* sweep over him as he ran over and stared down at the carnage.

Clint half expected the heretic to glance up at him longingly, but before Clint could test that theory, he fired the 1911 until it was empty. The lifeless heretic rolled off of Earl and the fat man smiled weakly and said, "Thank you." Then his chest heaved as he fainted again.

Earl's fat arm lay across the broken body of the heretic and it almost resembled an embrace.

SEVEN

TREACHERY

It requires more courage to suffer than to die.

~*Napoleon Bonaparte*

Chapter Twenty-Five
Dying On Your Back

COCKROACHES HAVE BULKY bodies composed of three heavy body segments which are only supported by six long, thin legs. As they die, they lose muscle control, causing the leg muscles to contract. As a result, the legs are pulled beneath the body causing them to lose their balance and topple over. Cockroaches tend to die on their backs.

Chapter Twenty-Six
Management

CLINT FOUND THE boy hogtied in a room that once might have been a bedroom, but it had long since deteriorated into filth and decay. The stench was overwhelming. The floors were littered with feces and the walls smeared with it. Several skeletal bodies were piled in a corner. The walls and ceilings were so covered with roaches that they pulsed, as if they shared a heartbeat. Clint imagined he had been swallowed by some ancient leviathan and the heartbeat belonged to it.

The boy was now no more than four years old, his face round and smooth and his body small and fragile. His eyes were red and snot had dried above his mouth. He stared up at Clint and asked, "Are you okay?"

"Sure," Clint said, then he spat a mouthful of blood against the floor. His tongue pressed against his teeth and he realized several of them were loose. "Forget me. Did those monsters hurt you?"

The boy shook his head and asked, "Did you kill them?"

Clint remained silent and slowly worked the knots loose and unbound the boy's wrists and ankles. Clint pulled the boy into his arms and said, "I did. I killed them. Close your eyes. I'm going to take you out of here."

The boy clung to Clint as tight as a baby opossum. Clint walked out past the dead heretics and carefully stepped over Earl.

Earl's eyes sprung open and he screamed, "Son of a bitch" and quickly crawled away from the dead heretic sprawled next to him. Earl reached back and felt the wound at his shoulder and asked, "How bad is it?"

Clint glanced down at the gory mess and said, "You'll live. It's mostly stopped bleeding."

Earl crawled over to a wall and pulled himself up to his foot and said, "Let's get out of here."

Earl hopped out into the hallway.

Clint followed and once they were outside he told the boy, "You can open your eyes now."

The boy opened his eyes, and when he saw Earl he cringed.

Earl waved his hand dismissively and said, "Don't worry about me. I'm not going to hurt you."

The boy buried his face in Clint's shoulder.

Clint stared at Earl and said, "I want out of here."

Earl shook his head and said, "Management isn't happy. I can feel its anger like shards of glass in my brain. You broke the rule."

"What are you talking about?" Clint shouted. "What rule?"

"You aren't allowed to kill the other tenants," Earl said. "When you killed Mr. Anderson it set off a chain reaction. Management was momentarily distracted and it only took a short time for the tenants up here to claw their way down. You caused all of this destruction around us."

"I don't understand."

Earl sighed and said, "The tenants up top have been here the longest. After a time, even suffering loses its flavor. They became something less than human—pests, if you will. You did Management a favor in ridding the complex of them and I certainly appreciate you saving my bacon. Of course, if you followed the rules they never could have gotten to me in the first place."

"You sent me up here," Clint said evenly. "Were you planning on them eating me?"

"Of course not," Earl said defensively. "You are the prized gem. Management would never have purposefully put you in danger. It was completely unexpected when you refused your room. Unprecedented."

"My room?" Clint said. "Why does Management want me?"

"You still don't know?" Earl asked. "I assumed that by now you would have remembered."

Clint's mind drifted to a bathtub filled with blood and he said, "I do remember."

Earl shook his head and said, "No, you don't."

Clint suddenly recalled the note the doctor wrote and he reached into his pocket, but instead of notebook paper, he withdrew a neatly folded newspaper clipping.

Clint carefully sat the boy down on the ground, read the newspaper, and he remembered.

PROBE FINDS THAT THE INFAMOUS BUG MAN MAY HAVE KILLED OVER 200 PEOPLE

Helen Freely—Lake Charles
Daily Sentinel, Saturday, 6 January 2013

AN UNKNOWN assailant ominously known as the Bug Man may have killed up to 235 unsuspecting victims, according to a chilling new investigation.

This year the substantiated deaths were of 18 people, but police suspect the death toll is substantially higher.

A yearlong review of the case uncovered a pattern of deaths that may have begun over two decades before they were detected. The findings exceeded even the wildest estimates of the death toll.

After confirmation of the initial 18 killings, police investigators gave the names of 23 additional people to the Federal Bureau of Investigation. They investigated 184 deaths before the inquiry was scaled down. The staggering figure makes the assassin possibly the United States' worst serial killer. Shockingly, as many as two-thirds of the victims are suspected to be elderly women.

The serial killer preyed on elderly, vulnerable women, murdering victims apparently by making visits to their homes under the pretense of performing pest control while actually poisoning their food. The deaths were eventually discovered after police exhumed the grave of an elderly woman after her relatives suspected foul play. Toxicology tests uncovered traces of cyanide, ironically a poison found in a variety of substances such as almonds, tobacco smoke, and pesticides. In lethal doses it is a rapid killer, with death occurring in one to fifteen minutes.

The investigation has not yet

pinpointed a suspect; however, the accepted theory is that the murderer poses as an employee of a pest control company in Louisiana (or possibly one of the surrounding states).

An emotional FBI agent described the "wicked, wicked crimes" as a chilling abuse of trust. "Each of the victims extended their trust. He (or she) murdered each and every one of his (or her) victims by a calculating and cold-blooded perversion of his duties. For his evil and wicked purposes he took advantage and grossly abused the trust each of his victims put in him. I have little doubt each of his victims smiled and thanked him as he performed his service."

Local coroner Stephen McMichael said he believed it was impossible to put a precise figure on the number of victims. The evidence suggests the murderer is obsessed with death and enjoys the power of life or death.

Detective Richard Flake said the murderer has a taste for killing.

Investigating officer, Detective Chief Inspector Michael Dean said, "He likes control and the ultimate control over life is inflicting death." It was a view also reached by forensic psychiatrist Rick Wick, who suggested the murderer kills to get rid of anxiety and is not comfortable unless he is in complete control. "The killer could either be in a state of complete control, in which case, he is relaxed and normal, or in a state of collapse. He is not doing it for excitement. He is trying to get rid of an anxiety, but an anxiety which he may not even let himself think about at the time."

The public is urged to contact authorities should they suspect any unusual activity and, in particular, regarding a pest control technician or someone posing as such.

Chapter Twenty-Seven
The Bug Man

CLINT FOLDED THE newspaper article and pushed it back into his pocket.

Clint remembered it all.

Had he ever truly forgotten?

Bug Man.

The boy had grown smaller, no more than a toddler now.

Earl forced a smile and asked, "Do you understand?"

"I'm a monster," Clint whispered.

"It's not your fault," the boy said softly. "You tried your best to avoid the stressors, but life caught up to you."

Clint stared at Earl and said, "And you wanted me to remember? You think this is better?"

"You bet," Earl said. "You have to suffer. Management feeds on it the way flowers need sunlight. It used to be summer in here year-round, back in the day, hundreds of suffering souls all packed in. That much suffering eventually builds its own body, becomes an entity all its own. Creation, just like a baby in its mother's womb."

"You keep referring to Management," Clint said. "What is it?"

Earl smiled, opened his arms and said, "It's all around us. The walls, the ceiling, the floor. The history. All of it."

"The asylum?" Clint asked.

"That's right," Earl agreed. "Only more than that. An asylum is dead, but Management is alive. It breathes and thinks and is constantly creating. Management wanted you and in its own way it called you here. It has a way of reaching into you. Eventually you'll hear its whispers more clearly and when it speaks to you, it's like the voice of God."

Clint gestured at the boy and asked, "Why is he here?"

Earl shrugged and said, "I have no idea. You brought him. I do know this much, Management must be delighted. Considering how you've broken the rule, that much at least is in your favor."

Clint turned to the boy and said, "I thought you were my . . . I thought you were Michael."

"No," the boy said.

Clint stared deeply into the boy's eyes and said, "You're me, aren't you? The child I was long before the world started burying me, one scoop at a time."

The boy nodded and said, "And I'm you."

Earl giggled and said, "What a beautiful family reunion. I've seen some twisted shit but never anything like this. Management feeds on two things: the energy from those who suffer and the energy from those who cause suffering. It takes that energy and manifests whatever it is that causes the most pain." Earl extended a hand to the child and said, "Nice to meet you, Clint."

The boy turned away.

"If he's Clint then what does that make me? The Bug Man?"

Earl smiled and said, "Exactly. Somehow you separated yourself: the victim and the predator."

"The exterminator," Clint corrected.

"The Bug Man," the child whispered.

"I still don't see how you've done it," Earl said, "but it's glorious. Two for the price of one."

"I have lots of practice," Clint said. "I'm schizophrenic."

"Excellent," Earl squealed. "Occupancy is low, and you've certainly contributed to the empty apartments, but you two are welcome additions. Management is pleased, and besides, the other rooms will fill up soon enough. Eventually the entire structure will be renovated and filled to capacity."

Clint shook his head and said, "We aren't staying. I've done some bad things, but I'm mentally ill and the boy . . . well, we don't deserve to be here."

Earl frowned. "Leaving isn't an option. The last one to try lived in Apartment 2."

Clint withdrew the 1911 from his satchel and said, "I'm making it an option. If need be I can start by killing you and then slowly work my way down. At what cost is Management willing to try to keep us?"

Enough.

The boy shuddered and Earl dropped down to the ground and bowed.

The commanding voice came from within and without; it was everywhere and nowhere.

Remember.

Clint closed his eyes and what he saw was Jenn sprawled out in a bathtub filled with her blood, the murky depths hiding their infant child.

"It wasn't my fault," Clint whispered, his eyes still tightly closed. "She did it."

Remember it all.

There was a note on the bathroom sink. Clint didn't want to read it again, desperate to leave it somewhere in the depths of his memory.

Remember.

In his mind's eye, Clint picked up a note written by his wife. Her last message to him before she killed herself and their son.

I know where you've been going at night and I know what you've been doing. I knew what I was getting myself into when I married you, but I hoped you could get better. Prayed for it. I never imagined what you would become. I blame myself for choosing you, but Michael is blameless. Innocent. He deserved better. Now, I stare at him and I realize he is poisoned. I imagine his future and the conclusion I always come to is that he will grow up and become just like you. I can't take that chance.

The Bug Man opened his eyes and he stared down at the boy; Clint was softly weeping.

A man is nothing more than what's been done to him and what he's done.

The Bug Man knew this to be true.

Chapter Twenty-Eight
Apartment 15

THE BUG MAN reached down, lifted Clint, and cradled his small, fragile body close to his chest and slowly walked down the hallway.

Behind them Earl giggled.

As they approached the middle of the hallway a descending staircase materialized and the Bug Man slowly walked down the pink stairs. The Bug Man covered the boy's eyes as the dead border collie came into view.

They stepped up to an unmarked apartment and the Bug Man opened the door and went inside.

The wall outside shifted and a 15 formed above the door.

The Bug Man closed the door behind them and stared at a framed photograph on the wall: he and his wife were curled up in a hospital bed. Jenn was pale and tired. A newborn child was wrapped in a blanket as tight as a burrito, eyes narrow and blue, face still red from the effort of being born. They held the child between them like a trophy.

Michael.

The Bug Man placed Clint on the ground and said, "Welcome home."

The Bug Man sat down in a green easy chair. Clint came to him, unzipped the satchel, and withdrew the prescription bottle of Risperdal. The Bug Man stared down at the child and said, "If I stop taking them, I'll lose my mind again. I'll be lost in a delusion."

Clint stared up at the Bug Man and said, "Wouldn't that be easier?"

The Bug Man nodded.

Clint walked into the bathroom and paused for a moment. He stared at the empty bathtub, and then he poured the Risperdal into the toilet and flushed it.

From the living room the Bug Man shouted, "Get me a drink."

Clint stuck his head into the living room and whispered, "What do you want?"

"Whiskey."

About the Author

Aaron T. Milstead is a novelist and short story writer as well as an English professor at Stephen F. Austin University. He owns Southeastern Pest Control and is a licensed exterminator. He lives deep within the Piney Woods of East Texas with his wife and three children.